Good Luck Babe

Z.E Lewis

Good Luck Babe playlist

- "Fake Nice" by The Aces
- "Bullshit on the Internet" by Suki Waterhouse
- "You Belong With Me (Taylor's Version)" by Taylor Swift
- "Too Slow" by Maude Latour
- "Pretty Girls" by Renee Rapp
- "girls" by girl in red
- "Cherry" by Harry Styles
- "Gorgeous" by Taylor Swift
- "Buzzcut Season" by Lorde
- "Treacherous" by Taylor Swift
- "Risk" by Gracie Abrams
- "Kaleidoscope" by Chapple Roan
- "If we lived on the moon" by vivi rincon
- "I Want To Be With You" by chole moriondo
- "Volcanic Love" by The Aces
- "Good Luck, Babe!" By Chappel Roan
- "Meantime" by Chappel Roan
- "I wanna be your girlfriend" by girl in red
- "Keep Driving" by Harry Styles
- "Ribs" by Lorde
- "Iris- Acoustic" by The Goo Goo Dolls
- "Machine" by Jensen McRae
- "Red Wine Supernova" by Chapple Roan
- "This Side of Paradise" by Coyote Theory
- "Long Live (Taylor's Version)" by Taylor Swift

To Zachary Lewis, for always listening to my stories.

This one's because of you.

"We are all heading for each other in a collision course, no matter what. Maybe some people are just meant to be in the same story."

—Jandy Nelson, *I'll Give You the Sun*

CAT

"Does my hair look okay?" I asked as I fixed my makeup.

"You look fine, hon," Mickey said from the bed.

"Can you check the back?"

He groaned and lifted Ginger off of his lap before moving over to me.

"You look fine," he repeated. "You look great, Cat." Mickey went back to my bed and put Ginger back onto his lap. Ginger is my cat. She's orange with black eyes.

"I only get one chance at these photos; I cannot screw this up," I said, checking that my eyeliner was correct. I'd done it four times before they both looked the same.

Today, I was taking my senior photos for cheer. The varsity team was meeting with our football team in the gym at seven thirty. Which meant Ryan was going to be there, so I'd have to see him for the first time in a month.

My hair was in two Dutch braids running down my back. Coach Roe came up with the style earlier this summer and made sure everyone knew how to do it.

I was in my new uniform. It was my favorite so far, a one-piece suit with the typical white-and-blue GO DOLPHINS cheer top sewed onto a teal skirt. It also had pockets. After our uniform last year caused one of our flyers to accidentally flash a crowd of people during a competition, we had to go in a different direction.

"You always look great in photos, Cat," Mickey said, taking photos of Ginger lying on him. "You've got nothing to worry about."

"Not always."

"We don't talk about freshman year."

We both bowed our heads in a moment of silence for that yearbook photo. I was a really shy freshman, and I didn't know a lot of people. I had yearbook photos after lunch and nobody told me I had a huge chunk of burger meat in my teeth until after the photo was in the yearbook. I almost moved schools. It would have been justified.

"Are you ready yet?" Mickey asked as he scrolled through his Instagram.

I rolled my eyes. Mickey and I had been friends since second grade when he moved here from Alabama. He didn't come out until he was thirteen and in middle school. He told me first, and then his mom and dad. They were both glad he told them, because they'd known for years. Apparently, the fact that he could sing every word of *The Sound of Music* by seven was a tip-off. His family had always been really supportive, and when he was sixteen, we all went down to River City Pride for the first time with him.

My parents knew, too. That was the only way he was allowed to spend the night at my house. We had sleepovers at each other's houses at least once a week because we lived on the same road, with my house on the corner and his at the end of the cul-de-sac.

"Yeah," I said, checking out my reflection one last time. I'd tanned a little over the summer, making my hair look even more blonde. I had on pink blush and matching lipstick. I wanted to look delicate.

"Great, 'cause I want coffee," Mickey said.

"Is that the only reason you're here?" I asked as I grabbed my tote bag and keys.

"Yes. I cannot stress that enough," Mickey deadpanned. "But, like, also here for emotional support."

"Yeah, right."

"Come on, who else would be here to tell you that you look amazing?"

I sighed as we left the house and got into my Honda. My grandmother gave it to me last year, after she bought herself a new Jeep. I drove us to The Treehouse, a coffee shop five minutes away from the school. It was the best hang-out place in town, and it had a drive-through.

"Welcome to The Treehouse, what can I get for you today?"

I placed our orders, and I ordered Ryan a coffee, too.

"You're so romantic, getting him coffee," Mickey teased. "What's next? The wedding?"

"Shut up," I groaned. I pulled up to the window, paid, and then handed Mickey the coffees.

Ryan and I were… complicated. He was amazing—the kind of guy Hallmark movies are based on. His parents were both kind and very successful. He loved his family and spent his weekends volunteering at the animal shelter. He fostered kittens over the summer. He was perfect.

But I never cared about him like he cared about me.

I parked in the cheer-captain parking spot. It was thrilling to finally park here after four years of waiting. When I started high school, I was on the pre-varsity team with a lot of the girls who were now on varsity. During sophomore year, Maddie, Veronica and I got onto the varsity team.

During my junior year, I made sure to market myself and get my name to the front of everyone's minds. I brought fruits to football games for the girls and Gatorade for the football team. I passed the idea of locker-decorating from Coach Roe to the principal, and it was a huge hit.

So, when the spot for cheer captain opened up, I was a shoo-in. Easily. I worked hard for this, so why didn't it feel right?

I stepped out of my car and reapplied my chapstick in my car window's reflection. I took a deep breath before getting my coffee from Mickey.

"Cat!" Maddie yelled as I stepped into the cool gym. It was a welcome relief from the sweltering heat outside.

I smiled and turned to her as she hugged me. "Hey, Mads!" I said, returning her hug while being careful not to spill my drink.

"How was PA?" Maddie's cheer uniform showed off her tattoos. She had traveled a lot with her dad before he retired to open a tattoo shop, and on the back of her legs were tattoos of the state birds of every state she had ever lived in. All of them were done by her or her family. They were made to last, with thick, black lines and no color. The largest was a northern mockingbird just above her left knee for her home state of Texas, but my personal favorite was New Mexico's roadrunner on her right ankle.

"Great," I said. I had spent the past month in Pittsburgh with my aunt, Becca, and her fiancée, Faith. Becca was twenty-five and Faith was twenty-three, which was kind of strange because of how close in age they were to me. All my other aunts and uncles were at least fifteen years my senior.

"We went to a thing called the Ohiopyle. It's a natural water slide that was carved through erosion into these rocks. Here, I have some photos, I posted about it," I said, showing her a few photos of Becca and me.

"Hannah didn't go?" Maddie asked. Hannah was my stepsister. She was only two years younger than me, and our parents moved in with each other when I was seven, so we were raised together.

"No, she had basketball camp." I took a sip of my coffee. "How was the NJROTC camp?"

"So fun!" Maddie's face lit up. "The camp was fantastic. Everyone was so nice and I got to attend and trainings workouts and everything, it was great."

"Are you going to apply?"

Maddie shrugged. “Probably not. It was amazing, but I wanna be reckless in my twenties. I wanna be able to take a flight to Mexico on a whim. I want to be able to skip class to see a concert. I can’t do that there.”

“Well, at least you know,” I said. “Your dad off your back about it now?”

“Surprisingly, yeah,” Maddie said. “He just wanted me to try it before I made up my mind. I came, I saw, I left. Oh, I see Ryan." She waved him down from across the gym as he stepped through the door.

Great.

I turned to Mickey and he handed me Ryan’s coffee as he walked up to us. Somehow, I forgot how tall Ryan was when I didn't see him every day.

Ryan was six foot two with broad shoulders and muscles like a Greek god. He had dark-brown skin and a fade; he cut off his dreadlocks when he joined the football team because they made him overheat.

He smiled at me like I was the only person in the room. I smiled back at him, wishing I was.

“Aw, thanks, baby!” Ryan said as I handed him his coffee. It looked small in his hand. He put his arm around my waist and I leaned into him as I sipped my coffee. I’m not short, but he was still almost half a foot taller than me.

“Ew, you’re too cute, it’s gross,” Maddie teased. Mickey nodded as he sipped his coffee.

“Hey, Mickey!” Ryan said, reaching out his hand for a fist bump. Mickey complied but gave me a “I’m only doing this because you’re dating him” look. I rolled my eyes.

"What'd you do this summer, man?"

"I just trained for cross-country, did some campus tours," Mickey said. "What about you?" Mickey was planning on going to the University of Alabama for cross-country. They had already offered him a large scholarship.

"Oh, y'know, kind of whatever," Ryan said. "I went to Haiti for a couple weeks to help rebuild this school that got destroyed by a hurricane."

"Y'know, casual stuff," I joked.

"You still want to go into education?" Mickey asked.

Ryan nodded. "Yeah, someone needs to," he said. "Plus, I love working with kids. I want to teach middle school. I feel like that's when kids learn morals the most and need a great role model. Even if I can't be that for them, I can help them find someone."

"You'd be a great role model," I said, looping my arm through his and resting my head on his shoulder. "I mean, you're, like, the perfect student."

"And boyfriend?" Ryan smirked. Guilt was like a kick to the stomach. Yes, he was the perfect boyfriend.

"Yes, that too." I kissed his lips, closing my eyes and trying not to think about how much of a liar I was.

I knew I didn't like men. I never have. At first, with Ryan, I thought I could.

It was the week before prom, and everyone was coordinating outfits with their dates. Mickey and I were going to go together because neither of us had been asked.

It started with Lisa making a joke. "God, Cat, you never seem to like any of the boys. What are you, a lesbian?" She laughed, and so did the rest of the team. I laughed, too.

"No, I just know about something called privacy, Lisa," I said. "I don't kiss and tell."

Perfect planning. Everyone thought I was secretly with men. Or, it was perfect, until Ryan asked me to prom. He did it in the best way, too.

It was sixth period on a Friday, and he came into class dressed in gym shorts and a cheer crop top. He had pom-poms, and one of his teammates had a speaker playing *You Belong with Me* by Taylor Swift. Ryan danced, shook his ass, and sang in front of the entire class. Words cannot describe how iconic it was. And then, his friend handed him flowers and a sign.

Cat, will you belong with me at homecoming?

What could I have done? Said no? It would have been clear that *I* was the problem. Everyone liked Ryan. I'm pretty sure half the men at school, even the straight ones, liked him. He was the Ryan Reynolds of our school. So, I was Blake Lively, I guess. When really, I was more like Kristen Stewart.

"Aaron Quinn!" the photographer called.

Ryan groaned and pulled away from me. "Sorry, I need to go get the team lined up."

"Yeah, I need to, too," I said. Ryan smiled and thanked me again for the coffee before running off.

"Squad!" I yelled. Most of the girls were talking to their boyfriends, but they all came to me.

"I'm going to go walk around campus," Mickey said, walking away. My eyes followed him, boring a hole into the back of his skull. Traitor.

"Squad," I said, turning back to everyone. "How was everyone's summer? Here, I'm going to pass my keys around. If you have the keys, it's your turn to talk."

We only had seven seniors on our varsity team. Maddie, Lisa and Zyaire were our flyers. Then, our bases, Miracle and me. Lastly, our spotters, Veronica and Del.

"I went on a missionary trip with my church to Mexico to help all of them," Lisa said, an air of unsubtle condescension whirling about her. She was a preacher's daughter, with long brown hair, honey eyes, and pale skin littered with freckles. "It's so sad, they're so unfortunate and poor. I saw this cute little kid; I wished I could bring him home with me!"

"Okay, Del, it's your turn," I directed. Her real name was Delia, but everyone called her Del. She talked about how she worked in the public library this summer for community service hours.

I tried to keep them all talking in a circle as we took turns getting our photos done. I wanted the squad to be more than a team. I wanted us to be a family.

"Remember, we have cheer camp next week," I said after the last of us had had their photo taken. "It's gonna be in the gym from nine a.m. to three p.m. Bring water and lunch."

"Can we keep these uniforms?" Zyaire asked.

"Great question," I said. "No, you must bring it back on Monday. Any other questions?"

"Nope," Miracle said, and everyone else echoed her.

"Great," I said. "If you need anything, check the group chat and if it's not already been posted, text me, and then Coach Roe. She's on vacation right now with her husband, we don't wanna disturb her if we don't have to."

"Aye, aye, Captain," Maddie saluted me with a wink. I rolled my eyes but smiled. Captain. Hell yeah.

"Okay, squad dismissed!" I cheered. Everyone went their separate ways. Maddie and I walked out to the parking lot and found Mickey lying on the hood of my car.

"That took forever!" he whined, with all the drama of a toddler whose parent ran into an old friend at the grocery store.

"You could have gone to your house," I said.

Mickey shrugged. "Free coffee."

"What are you gonna be doing today?" Maddie asked me.

"Sleeping," I said. "But after lunch I'm gonna hang out in the pool with Mick."

"Can I come over? I'm so bored at home."

"Yeah, do you need a ride?"

"No, I'll drive over at twelve thirty, that work?"

"Yeah," Mickey said. "We'll be awake by then."

"Cool. Good seeing ya, Captain." Maddie hugged me before getting into her car. I got into mine and drove away.

"Seven is too early for anything." Mickey sprawled himself over my bed.

I lay down, too, and looked out my bedroom window as Mickey napped. My brain was moving too fast to allow me any peace.

I could tell Mickey about the Ryan situation. He'd be fine with it; I know he would. Sure, he made the occasional joke about masc lesbians, but he wasn't homophobic.

My biggest concern with him was that he'd question it. He'd ask if I was sure and how long I knew and a million other questions. If I couldn't answer all of them perfectly, I'd feel like I was making it up. I didn't know how long I knew; it wasn't a sudden realization that I liked women. It was more the slow realization that I didn't like men.

I just didn't see the point in coming out. It's not like I was in love with anyone. Sure, I'd had the occasional crush on girls in my classes, but they were all straight. I could wait until I was in college and could be out and proud and shit. I could cut my hair and dye it pink. I could date whoever I wanted once I was in college.

Right now, coming out just put too much at risk. It could wait. I was fine playing Ryan's perfect, straight girlfriend.

And it would cause so much drama with Lisa. She already made jokes about me being gay. She talked shit about theater kids and pitched a fit when she found out the new band director had a husband instead of a wife.

Imagine if she knew I liked girls. She would call for me to be removed as captain, and I don't know who would stick up for me.

This was easier. I could be happy with Ryan. I could try.

ANDI

I spaced out as I stared at my reflection. Today was the first day of senior year, and I needed everything to be perfect.

I'd woken up at five thirty to go on a jog with Poppy (my German Shepard), shower, do yoga, and make myself poached eggs for breakfast. I loved getting up early because nobody else in the house was awake. Peter was just now waking up, and Mom and Dad didn't have to be up for hours.

"Come on, man," I said, knocking on Peter's door.

"I'm up," he groaned from inside. Of course, he'd forgotten to set an alarm.

I rolled my eyes. "Want coffee?"

"Yeah."

I went into the kitchen and poured some into his *Star Wars* thermos. He was only a year younger than me, but from how he acted, you'd think there was at least a five-year age gap. Or maybe it's from how I acted. I'd always been told I was mature for my age. It was a kind way of saying I had shitty parents.

They moved all the time because of their job. Mom was an engineer and Dad was a contractor. They worked for the same company and got moved at least once every other year. I hated it. On the bright side, they swore that they would stay in one place for my senior year, and we just moved from Tampa to Jacksonville, so I still qualified for in-state tuition.

Once I graduated, I wanted to go to college to study... something. I wasn't sure what I wanted to do yet. Mom and Dad were pushing for law school, but I was pretty sure they just wanted to brag that their daughter was a lawyer. Same reason they were pushing Peter for med school.

I wanted a big house that was all mine. I wanted to be able to paint the walls and hang up posters because I owned it. I wanted to be able to replace the shitty carpet in the living room. I wanted a garden, with flowers and life all around the house.

I filled up Poppy's water before taking Peter to school. We listened to a country radio station I liked on the way there. Today was going to be a good day.

I was going to make it a good day.

"See ya," Peter mumbled as he put his headphones on and left the car. I rolled my eyes and pulled out my phone to double-check my schedule. Sadly, I ended up with a full six classes this year. My first class, AP Lit, started in twenty minutes. I really liked reading, so I was glad it was AP Literature and not AP Language; I was a shit writer. Then, I had theater. I joined it on a whim, figuring it might be fun. I was in trig, chemistry, US government, and an extra European history class.

I joined theater because I loved movies. I've never acted, but it seemed like it could be fun. I follow a bunch of TikTok acting accounts and I really liked watching them. At least with the class, I'll know what they're saying is real.

By the time I got to class, all the seats in the back had been taken. Just my luck. I sat in the front, crossing my arms over my chest. I looked around the classroom, but I didn't recognize anyone.

I wish I could say I was super popular at my old school, but I was the kid who sat in the back of class listening to music and drawing. I studied a lot, so I passed all my classes, but the whole 7 a.m.-class thing never worked for me. I learned more studying at 12 a.m. than I did sitting in class at 12 p.m.

"Phones away," the teacher, Mr. Matthews, said. He had dark black hair and looked young. I bet this was his first-year teaching.

I never understood why people went into teaching. Why would you want t to spend most of your life in a school? I spent most of my day dreaming about being out of school.

He was dressed well, too, in a blazer and ironed pants. Who wears a blazer to a public school?

I tossed my phone into my backpack and took out my well-loved copy of *Last Night At The Telegraphy Club.* It was one of my favorite books.

"As this is a senior class, I'm going to rely on you to pace yourselves," he said, sitting on his desk. "Each quarter, we will read a different book, and you'll have to complete a twenty-five-page study guide." The entire class groaned.

"You may work in groups no larger than four people," Mr. Matthews said. "We'll be doing checks every other week to ensure that actual progress is being made and so that I can put in a grade for something."

The girl behind me raised her hand, and I turned to look at her. She was… stunning. She had long blonde hair and light-blue eyes. Her face was round and she had high cheekbones that I swear had a little glitter on them. She looked like sunshine personified.

"Do we have to work in groups, or can we do this individually?" she asked. I decided I liked this girl.

"Yes, you have to work in groups," Mr. Matthews said. "I want you to have other people's opinions on the book."

"Which is?" I asked, not bothering to raise my hand.

"We'll be reading *Atonement* by Ian McEwan," Mr. Matthews said.

Some boy in the back raised his hand. "Ain't there a movie of it?"

"No," Mr. Matthews lied. I smiled at that. "Okay, you have the rest of class to pick your partners. Before class is over, grab your copy of the book and a study guide from my desk. One for each person in the group," he clarified as the boy in the back started to raise his hand again.

I turned around to the girl behind me.

Her grin made my breath catch. "Hi," she said. "I don't recognize you, are you new?"

"Yeah," I said, brushing my hair over my shoulder. It was dyed red, but my brown roots were starting to grow back. "I'm Andrea, but everyone calls me Andi."

"I'm Catherine, but everyone calls me Cat," Cat said. "I like your hair."

"Thanks," I said, blushing a little at the compliment. Mom and Dad hated the color. Then again, they hate me dying my hair in general. "Wanna work together? I would rather do it by myself too, so this way at least we're not stuck with… extroverts," I said, pretending to be horrified and holding my hand over my chest.

Cat laughed. "Sounds good!"

CAT

I had a study period, so I headed up to the library to look at *The Grapevine*, an anonymous gossip blog that was updated weekly. I was sure she had posted something this morning, spilling any secrets she collected over the summer.

Nobody knew who ran *The Grapevine*. She wasn't picky enough about drama to give away which cliques she hung out with. She wrote about band kids, theater kids, athletes, and NJROTC equally. The school tried to stop her, but nobody was able to discover who she was.

She was the main reason why Ryan and I were dating. There was a post made before prom last year, featuring a picture of me and Maddie at a football game. It was a bad angle. We were trying to talk, but it was so loud I had to lean in. The post questioned whether our relationship was purely platonic or if I was gay.

Dating Ryan let me shoot down that rumor. As the main writer and chief editor of *Fresh Off the Press* (the school newspaper), I created a column for couples who wanted to announce their relationship status and used it to report on mine before *The Grapevine* could attack me again.

The column was still running, though, due to the school's policy, we could only write about straight relationships. We were never explicitly told that we couldn't feature queer couples, but the principle encouraged us to only pick couples that were "family-friendly" and that "supported our local Christian values."

I pulled up *The Grapevine* on a library computer. There was an article about the summer breakups and hook-ups, complete with candid photos. Nothing too shocking or dramatic.

I pulled up my email and messaged Ms. Livingstone—the newspaper's sponsor—asking if I could do an interview on Andi for the blog. She responded within ten minutes, saying it was a great idea. I would need to find Andi and get her number.

Andi was gorgeous. She was wearing tight black jeans that hugged every curve of her hips on a way that made me want to run my hands along them. Her dark blue tank top was tight along her chest and tucked into her jeans. Her bra was visible in a unashamed, prideful way which made me wonder what she looked like without one.

She also had on silver jewelry, which I noticed was a nice complement to her pale skin. She was slightly suntanned on her shoulders and nose, but mostly her skin was as pale as porcelain. She reminded me of a statue of Venus with all its curves and perfections. I could spend all day memorizing every inch of her appearance and I wouldn't get bored.

Andi also had piercings. She had an eyebrow piercing and three ear piercings in each ear. She looked badass.

The fact that she was breathtaking and obviously queer had nothing to do with the fact that I needed to get her number. It was for the interview. Obviously.

ANDI

I sat in the back in my theater class. I made sure to get there as fast as I could and grabbed my hoodie from my backpack. I pulled it over my head, hoping to hide in it. I should have given that Cat girl my phone number. Or asked for hers. She was really pretty. I wondered if she was gay. I thought so, but maybe—

"Hey!" the teacher said as the bell rang, interrupting my thoughts. "Everyone, take your seats. Since it's the first day, you're gonna have an easy assignment. We're gonna be pairing up and writing a page—yes, a single page, how evil of me—about the movies or shows you watched over the summer."

I groaned. I didn't want to pair up, so I sat quietly, hoping the teacher, Ms. Bleacher, wouldn't notice me. But of course, she did. "Hey, I've never seen you before. Are you new to theater, or the school?"

"Both," I mumbled, leaning back in my seat. "I can write this assignment by myself—"

"Nonsense," Ms. Bleacher said, flagging down a trio of seniors from the other side of the classroom. "I said pairs."

Each student looked very different. There was a taller guy with a neon-green buzz cut who looked Asian American. He was dressed in a crop top and jeans with chains hanging on them. The other student was shorter, with ginger hair and freckles. She was wearing tan pants and a white polo with a navy-blue cardigan. The third person had short, curly black hair and darker skin, like they were Hispanic. They were the tallest, but only by an inch or so, and dressed in cargo shorts and a Hawaiian button-up.

"We're just catching up," the green-haired guy said.

"I know you all have phones because I've confiscated them before for texting each other during class. You could have done that over the summer," Ms. Bleacher said. "Rowan, you're gonna be with… Sorry, I forgot your name."

"Andrea," I said. "But everyone calls me Andi."

"Cool," Rowan said, sitting on the empty desk across from me. "I'm Rowan, pronouns they/them. This is Jordan"—they gestured at the tallest one—"they look like a dad, and not in a hot way. And this is Alex," Rowan said, pointing at the shortest of the group. "If you don't mind me asking, what are your pronouns?"

"She/her," I answered. I forgot how queer theater was. "I like your hair."

"Thanks," Rowan said. "It's the result of a bad break-up."

"We told you not to date him," Alex reminded them before turning to me. "So, Andi, where're you from?"

"I was born in Boston," I said. "But I moved here from Tampa."

"Navy brat?" Jordan asked.

"No, my parents work with a construction company, so they move a lot," I said. "You?"

"My mom retired from the Navy my freshman year," Jordan said. "Jacksonville is a big Navy area 'cause of the base. As someone who moved around a lot, you'll fit in here. People are pretty cool to the new kids."

"Thanks," I said, shrugging off my hood.

Rowan smiled. "Badass hair."

I smiled back at them. "Thanks," I said. "So, movies, right?"

We ended up talking about dozens of different shows and movies. By the end of class, Rowan had gotten my phone, compared our schedules, and invited me out to get ice cream with the three of them after school.

CAT

I ran into Andi at lunch. We were both waiting in line for cheeseburgers, which I swear were boiled in grease instead of cooked. She was ahead of me, but I recognized her hair.

"Hey," I said, tapping her shoulder.

She took her headphones off and scowled before she saw me and smiled a little. "Hey, Cat, what's up?"

"I'm with the school's newspaper," I said. "Can I have your number for an interview?"

"What?" She looked confused. "Why the hell would I need to do an interview?"

"Well, y'know," I said, feeling my cheeks heat up. *Because then I can get to know you better.* "You're the new kid, and it'd be cool."

"No thanks, babe," Andi said. "Not really the type to have an article written about them in a newspaper."

I thought back to a girl I knew sophomore year named Angelica. A rumor broke out about her having a surgery over the summer. Everyone spent the first week back at school wondering what happened. I knew she had gotten her appendix removed, so I asked to interview her and write an article on her surgery. She said no.

The next week, *The Grapevine* wrote that Angelica had gotten an abortion. It wasn't true, and they had no evidence, but it didn't matter. Everyone believed it.

I couldn't let that happen to Andi. We only just met, but I still felt a need to protect her. Maybe it was selfish, me wanting to repent for failing Angelica. But if it helped her, did it matter how selfish the motive was?

"Okay," I said. "But, just so you know, if *The Grapevine* gets to your story first, they'll say whatever they want, and anything we release will have to challenge it." I'd been dealing with *The Grapevine* for years. I knew how to play their games, even if I wished they didn't get to make the rules.

"What's *The Grapevine*?" Andi asked as the lunch lady handed her a plate.

"It's a gossip blog," I explained, being handed my own. "And they're good, really good. But they usually stay away from stuff that I write about first. So, if you do the interview, I can probably stop them from starting any rumors about you."

"Got me stuck between a rock and a hard place, babe."

"Pretty much everyone in the school reads *The Grapevine*. I'm just trying to help." I went to pay for lunch with my ID card, and our hands brushed. Her skin was so soft, I bet she didn't have a single callus. The touch ended as quickly as it had happened. "I can write the story and get it released by Wednesday."

"I can't meet today. I'm going out with some… people."

"Tomorrow, then," I said, handing her my phone. Her black nails stood out against the baby-blue phone case as she entered her phone number.

“This works out well, I wanted to give you my number anyways." She winked, turning. "See you around, Cat.”

It was her first day at a new school. I should have invited her to sit with us. So what if Lisa made a joke about her hair or something? Andi seemed like the type to have thick skin. I took a step after her, but then some ginger girl waved her down, and Andi turned to go with her.

Cool. She’d already made friends. I mean, who wouldn’t want to be her friend?

I went over to my table. Ryan had saved me a seat.

“Hey, Cat!” He kissed my cheek as I sat down next to him. Maddie and Veronica whistled, making me blush.

I smiled like normal as Veronica joked about this guy that struck out with her when she went to the beach on Sunday. Ryan’s friends came over and they all started talking about some video game I’d never heard of.

I wondered what Mickey was doing right now. He usually didn’t hang out with the football team. They’d made jokes about him for years. They teased him about his voice, hair, clothes, nails. Anything they deemed "too gay." I’d insisted to Mickey that they were just joking and that none of them were actually homophobic, but Mickey still stayed away. I understood why.

Ryan was the only one who never made fun of him. He’d always been really nice to Mickey and tried his best to make Mickey feel comfortable and included.

I wondered what Andi was doing. Was she making jokes with her friends? Was she thinking about the interview? What was she doing after school? Did she like me?

Ryan put his arm around my waist, spooking me out of my thoughts of Andi. I was a terrible girlfriend.

ANDI

"Rowan!" Jordan screamed as Rowan swerved between three lanes to make a nearly missed turn.

"Stop yelling!" Rowan shouted back, slamming the breaks at a stop sign and forcing Alex and I to brace ourselves on the backs of their seats.

"I am never driving with you again!"

"That's what you said last time, bitch, but you still ain't got a fucking car!" Rowan snapped back.

"I have my damn license!" Jordan said. "I can drive this piece of shit better than you can!"

"Don't call her a piece of shit! She's elderly, that's a protected class, fucker," Rowan said, slowly turning into the ice cream place. It was called Poodle's Ice Creamery. A large neon sign showed a white poodle eating strawberry ice cream.

"You two fight like an old married couple," Alex groaned as we all got out of the car. "Sorry about them, Andi. You'll get used to it, they're always like this."

"Not always," Jordan said.

"We get along sometimes." Rowan shared a knowing smile with Jordan. Alex rolled her eyes.

"Are you two together?" I asked. At lunch, I had thought that Alex and Jordan might have been dating. But maybe I was wrong.

"You're gay, right?" Rowan asked, prompting Alex and Jordan to slap their arms. "Hey!"

"You can't just ask someone if they're gay," Alex chastised, before turning to me. "Are you?"

"Yeah," I said. "Not big on label's though, usually just say queer."

"That's fine," Jordan said. "I'm demi."

"Anyway," Rowan said. "I was asking you to let you know that we're poly. I'm dating Jordan and Jordan's dating Alex."

"Oh," I said. "Cool."

"Rowan and I are not dating," Alex said. "I just felt the need to put that out there."

"You wish you could tap this," Rowan joked, putting their hands on their hips.

"Not in a million years," she laughed. "So, Andi, how was your first day?" Why was she always bringing the attention back to me?

"God, you're such a mom," Rowan teased, making me laugh. Alex rolled her eyes.

"Hey, what ice cream do you want?" Jordan asked, coming to stand beside me while Alex and Rowan bickered. I looked at the menu painted on the outside of the parlor.

"I'm gonna try the salted-caramel–cappuccino cone," I said. It was a limited-edition ice cream. I figured, why not?

"Good choice," Jordan said. "I'm gonna get the peach cobbler. Alex will get the brownie batter, and Rowan will get the Superman because they are a fucking child with no taste in ice cream."

"How did you two start dating?" I asked. "You and Rowan, I mean. You two seem so different."

"Yeah," Jordan said, smiling as they looked over to where Alex was reading at the menu and Rowan was vaping. "We've all been friends since we were little. I've known Rowan the longest, but I've still known Alex since we were 10. And then, near the end of sophomore year, Alex and I started… getting closer, and we started dating over the summer.

"Then Rowan started getting really jealous, and I thought it was because they wished I was hanging out with them more, but it turned out they just liked me. And then I freaked out and texted Alex and we spent, like, 6 hours one night on the phone talking about my feelings for Rowan until I realized I liked them, too. And then we spent more time talking about how this would affect Alex and I's relationship. And we came to our agreement. I've been seeing them for over a year now."

"I can't imagine that," I said. "I suck at relationships."

"Yeah, it's not meant for everyone," Jordan said as Alex came over and asked us if we were ready to order. Jordan was right about their partners' orders. Afterwards, we went to a few wooden picnic tables set up beside the Poodle to eat our ice cream.

I was comfortable around them. Their dynamic wasn't simple, but it was clear they loved each other very much. I'd never been in love. I didn't much care for relationships. They were too complicated, too messy. Loving someone was like carving out your own heart, holding it out to them and praying they wouldn't crush it. Plus, it's not like I had the best role models in my family for any big romance.

We must have been there for an hour before I got a text from Peter asking when I was coming back. I'd given him the car keys and let him drive himself home today. Still, I always came home when Peter asked.

"Hey, when are we going? My little brother just asked," I said, raising my phone as an explanation.

"Yeah, I need to get home, too," Alex said. We got our stuff together and headed back to the car. Rowan begrudgingly handed Alex the keys and sat in the back with me. They talked the entire way home about a design project they were doing in one of their classes. I was the closest house, so they dropped me off first.

I let myself in as quietly as possible. The house was silent. I hated silence. I would rather spend twenty-four hours a day in a car with Rowan talking nonstop than be in a silent house. I took off my shoes and headed to my room, shutting my door and blasting music through my headphones.

CAT

I texted Andi Tuesday morning to ask when she wanted to do the interview. She texted back that we could stay after school in the library, or another teacher's classroom. I sent her Ms. Livingston's room number.

I got there right after school and cleaned up a bit. The janitors usually only swept once a week, so I did today. I didn't want Andi to meet me in a dirty room.

I'd spent almost an hour picking an outfit and doing my makeup. Having matching eyeliner was much harder than it looked online. I finally decided on a white, slim-fit tennis dress with a light-blue hoodie over it. My makeup was light, with pink blush and lipstick. I wanted to seem down-to-earth and relaxed, even though I was pretty sure people who really were didn't spend an hour trying to be.

My heart jumped when someone knocked on the door, and I rushed over to open it. Andi was in green shorts and a black tank top and had tied a black flannel around her waist. Somehow, she was even more stunning than she was this morning.

"Hey, Cat," she said as she stepped in and looked around the room. "How do you know Ms. Livingstone?"

"She was my freshman-year English teacher," I said, walking over to the desks I had pushed together. Andi followed quietly.

"I've been a part of the book club and newspaper for over three years now. She sponsors them. What clubs are you in?"

"None, as of now." She sat down across from me. "Last year I was in my school's GSA for a couple weeks, but then everyone started dating each other, so I dropped out."

"What's GSA again?" I asked. "I've heard of it, but I just can't remember."

"Gay Straight Alliance," Andi said. "Although, my school called it the Gender and Sexuality Alliance, which didn't make a lot of sense. Then again, nobody in it was straight, and only three people were cis."

"Our school has something like that," I said. "Although, from what I remember, it only has four members."

"Really? My old one had, like, thirty," Andi said. "But we also based the meeting times off of the theater schedule so people could do both."

"Were you in theater?"

"Not that type of gay, babe," Andi smirked. I froze. She said it. She said she was gay. I mean, I was pretty sure, but she said it. Even Mickey didn't talk or joke about being gay. He was out, but in a well-kept secret sort of way. Nobody could mistake him for straight, due to his voice and how he dressed, but nobody caught him with any men or heard him talk about it either.

"Shit, did I make you uncomfortable?" Andi asked, making me realize I had gone silent. What would a straight person say to that?

"I have a friend that's gay," I blurted out, feeling heat rush to my face. Really? Well, at least that sounded straight.

"Good for you," Andi said, raising her eyebrows. "Anyway, wanna start the interview? Or was all of that on record, because—"

"We can start the interview now." I reached for my phone and turned on the recorder. "Are you aware this is being recorded?"

"Yes," Andi answered, leaning over the device.

"You don't need to do that," I said, stifling a laugh. "It detects noise very well. Could you state your first and last name and spell them?"

"My name is Andrea McCaffery," Andi said before spelling it. "Most people just call me Andi."

"Why is that?"

"My little brother started it when we were young and it's just stuck," Andi said. "The only people who still call me Andrea are my parents when they're pissed."

"Where all have you lived?" I asked. "And why do you move so often?"

"It's for my parents' job," Andi said. "I was born in Boston, and I guess I lived there till I was three, but I can't remember it. Then we lived in California, Washington, Nebraska, South Dakota, Vermont, and Alabama, and we've been in Florida for the last three years."

"What's your favorite place you've lived in?" I asked. She was so cool. She was funny, and well-traveled, and just so beautiful. I didn't notice it before, but she had little freckles on her nose and cheeks, and her eyes were a mossy shade of green.

"Probably California," Andi answered.

"Do you have any siblings or pets?"

She nodded. "I've got a German Shepherd named Poppy. She's six years old. And a younger brother, he goes to this school. He's a junior," Andi said, before whispering, "Do I have to say his name?"

"No," I answered. "What music do you like?"

This went on for almost an hour, just me asking questions. I wanted to get to know her better, and the interview was the perfect excuse because she didn't need to know anything about me.

"Well, that concludes our time," I said, stopping the recording on my phone. "Thanks again for coming here."

"Yeah, no problem," Andi said. "We should switch it up some time. You should let me interview you."

"I'm an open book, Andi," I lied. "You can ask me anything you want, anytime."

"I'll keep that in mind, babe," Andi said. I tried to move my hair over my face so she wouldn't see how red it was. Judging by her grin as she walked out, I failed.

ANDI

"You did what?" Peter yelled as I drove us to school on Wednesday.

"It's one newspaper article!" I reasoned. "And it's a school newspaper, who even reads it?"

"This writer better be really hot for you to do something as stupid as this just to hang out with her!"

I smacked him across the arm. "I didn't do it because she's hot, I did it to help her because she's been nice to me. She seemed excited about it, she even made a whole pitch." Also, if *The Grapevine* researched me, I knew what they would find, and I couldn't risk anyone finding out about what happened at my old school. "Have you made any friends?"

"It's only the third day, god, Andi," Peter groaned. "You're not Mom."

I rolled my eyes. Peter put on his headphones and stared out the window as I turned on the radio.

When I pulled into a parking spot, Peter all but jumped out of the car and hurried over to a group of people waiting outside of the school. At least he was talking to someone. I surveyed the group for a bit. Nobody was vaping, which was good; I didn't want Peter doing that. Nobody had any visible tattoos or piercings, either. God, I really was turning into—

"Hey!" Rowan was tapping on my driver's side window. I jumped, and they laughed before circling the car to sit in the passenger seat. "So, what're you doing?"

"Don't you know it's polite to ask before you get into someone's car?" I sighed. "I'm looking at my brother's friends, do you know them?" I pointed them out. Peter was leaning against the side of the school, in front of the basketball court. Almost a dozen other kids were around him, all wearing hoodies and gym shorts as if it was a uniform.

"Nope," they said. "Then again, it's probably a green flag that I don't. I mostly hang out with bad influences. Besides you, Jor and Alex."

"Thanks," I said, not sure if it was a compliment or insult. "Do you have any siblings?"

"Kinda?" Rowan shrugged. "I've been in foster care since I was eleven, and I've lived with other foster kids, but it's more like a roommate situation than a family one. Like, I don't talk to anyone from my first or second house."

I didn't know how to respond, so I just nodded quietly.

"My foster parents are pretty nice, though," Rowan added. "I never need or want anything. They're chill and they care about me. They support my hair and my gender and all that stuff. They even invite Jordan and Alex to family events."

"They seem cool," I said.

"What about your parents?"

"They are perpetually too busy," I answered honestly, but I didn't want to go into detail about them. I was all too aware that their idea of a happy marriage wasn't what everyone thought of. That most kids had never seen their parents fistfight, that most kids had never watched their dad almost drive into a tree while screaming at their mom. I knew most marriages didn't involve threats of assault charges. I didn't like talking about it.

It was always the same. First, it was pity. That went away after I didn't indulge it. Then, confusion, and questions. Lastly, people didn't care. They figured I was well adjusted to it, so I was fine. Which I was. I could be, when I needed to.

"Sounds fun," Rowan said. "House to yourself all the time. Bet you get laid a bunch."

"What the hell?" I asked, laughing. "No, what part of me makes you think I'm a… player?"

"Well, you're pretty hot and you've got a whole new-kid thing going on here. Like, you give big black-cat vibes. Really appealing."

"Whatever, babe," I said. "Why can't classes start at eight? Waking up at six is gonna be the death of me."

"Felt that."

"Hey, gays," Jordan said, opening my door and making jump again. "Time to get to class. Stop flirting."

"Do any of you ask before messing with someone's car?" I asked, stepping out. Alex stood next to Jordan, dressed in tan pants and an off-white button-up shirt. Jordan wore what appeared to be swim trunks and a wife beater.

"You going to the art show or a beach?" Rowan asked, as if reading my mind.

"Whatever, *Black Parade*," Alex said, rolling her eyes. Rowan was in a My Chemical Romance crop top and skinny jeans with silver chains on the hip.

"I look hot as hell," Rowan joked. "Right, Jor?"

Jordan looked Rowan up and down. "You look better in less," they said, making Rowan blush. Alex and I laughed as they walked ahead of us to class.

"So, how'd the interview go?" Alex asked, linking her arm through mine as we walked.

I shrugged. "Could have been worse," I said. "Cat was nice." But as we entered the school, I noticed people were staring at me. Too many people.

I realized then that I'd never asked Cat to send me the article before she posted it. What did everyone know that I didn't? What did she write about me?

CAT

Cheer practice started with a one-mile run around the track, after we stretched. Maddie and I jogged together. Once everyone finished, we all went to grab our waters.

"I read your article," Maddie said. I beamed. People loved it. It was shorter, only a page long, about Andi and how unique she is for moving right before her senior year. I think I even called her brave.

"Yeah, I read it too. Sounded like a dude wrote it," Veronica said. "It didn't give the drama it could have, like if *The Grapevine* did it."

"You ran straight into the point there, Ronnie," I said, rolling my eyes. "It's a high school newspaper, not a gossip blog."

"Clearly," Miracle said. "But Ronnie's right, *The Grapevine* has so many more views. You could take a page out of their book."

"Hey, this is still a big increase in views for *Fresh Off the Press*," Maddie argued.

"I don't know why you did it on a dyke and didn't bring that up," Lisa said. "If you mentioned her being gay, more people would have read it."

"Probably," I said, desperately wanting to chastise Lisa for calling Andi a dyke. "She didn't say anything about it." At least I could lie for her.

"Don't ask, don't tell, I guess," Maddie mumbled. She wouldn't be loud about it, but her older brother was bi and had been dating a really nice guy for the last three years. I knew people like Lisa bothered her, but she always did her best not to show it.

Maddie moved with a power that drew me in. She walked with her shoulders back and her head held high, like she knew she was the smartest person in any room she was in. She usually was.

It wasn't arrogance, though. She had a subtle, clever charm about her. She could fit in anywhere, and she posed corrections as questions. Instead of just telling people they were wrong, she'd say, "Really? I thought it was this way," and lead them to amend themselves.

And she took pride in her appearance, always taking care to brush out her long, black hair and contour the natural roundness of her face to appear sharper. Her eyes were dark as coal, and I could swear they sparkled when she grinned. I loved that sparkle.

"Everyone's gonna wanna talk to her," Lisa said, putting her water on the ground. "You should have said she was a dyke so the guys don't get their hopes up."

"Don't know, Lisa," I said. "Though she does look like one. Especially with the dyed hair. That alone should turn away men."

As soon as the words left my mouth, I felt Maddie's eyes on me. It was a joke, surely she'd understand. Maddie had to know I didn't really think like Lisa or Veronica. If I agreed with them, they'd be quiet. I just wanted them to shut up.

But they hadn't made me say it. I chose to.

"I tried talking to her in one of my classes," Del said. "She was short and kinda rude. I bet that'd turn them away too."

"So, we have nothing to fear!" Lisa joked. "If her appearance doesn't scare men away, her personality will!" Everyone laughed at this. I did too, but I felt like I was betraying a part of myself.

"Girls!" Coach said, storming across the field. "You know you're not allowed to gossip! You cannot just stand here and insult someone behind their back. Another mile lap, all of you. Everyone who just got here, you run too."

Coach Roe caught my arm before I could leave. "Hey, as the Captain, you need to shut that down. If you can't, I'll get someone who will. Understand?"

"Yes ma'am," I said, avoiding her eyes. I ran by myself for the last mile, imagining I was running away from anyone who thought like Lisa or Miracle or Ronnie. They were my friends, but would they still be if they knew the real me? If they knew how I really felt about Maddie and Andi? Would they ever look at me the same?

No, they wouldn't. And I'd be a captain that nobody respected or listened to. And then I'd be done. Years of work, for nothing.

I ran and tried to focus on my breathing and the track under my feet and the sun on my back and the terrible smell of the freshly fertilized football field. I let myself fall into the role of Captain Cat, perfect girlfriend and cheerleader, instead of who I really was. A dyke, as Lisa would say.

ANDI

"Hey, I'm Veronica." A girl had approached me while I was walking to my fifth-period US government class. She was tall, with long black hair, and she evidently had no respect for the rules of social propriety or human decency.

"Hi?" I said, taking off my headphones and trying to remember why she was talking to me. Should I know her? Did we talk earlier? She looked kinda familiar. It was weird having everyone want to talk to me; I didn't like the attention.

"I wanted to ask if you were coming to my back-to-school party," Veronica said. "I'll send you my address on Insta, but it's gonna be awesome. Only seniors are invited."

"Sorry, that's—"

"We're going!" Rowan said, jumping into existence beside me. They were like a fucking cat.

"Fantastic! Can't wait!" Veronica said, and then she skipped (skipped!) away. Like a goddamn Disney character.

"Parties ain't really my thing, babe," I mumbled as I put up my chem textbook and pulled out my government one from my locker.

"This'll be great, all of us can go together," Rowan said. "It's been so long since I've been to a party."

"Four weeks," Alex corrected, walking up to us with Jordan.

"Which is very long," Rowan complained.

"We also had that party for Jor's birthday two weeks ago," Alex said.

"That doesn't count," Rowan said, waving it off. "It was the three of us, plus Jor's family. It's what we would have done any other Friday night, but with presents and cake."

"You're just excited to get drunk," I teased.

"Hey, I don't drink," Rowan said. "But I do love watching people get drunk. It's the best thing ever. Andi, we gotta go. Have you ever seen two football players try to sing *Just Give Me A Reason* by P!NK?" They wiped fake tears from their eyes. "It's amazing. It's beautiful. It's lifesaving. If everyone saw that once in their lives, the suicide epidemic would be over."

"Okay," I said. People had always told me I needed to come out of my shell. I had always imagined it would be like opening a birdcage, but it turned out to be more similar to running over a turtle with a car and then using a spork to separate its shell from its insides.

"Great!" Rowan said, throwing their arms over my shoulders. They smelled like Axe body spray, and I really wanted to push them off, but I didn't.

"Rowan, give her some space," Alex said. She must have noticed how uncomfortable I looked. I silently thanked her. She smiled at me, so I think she got it.

"Come on, we're gonna be late for class. Again," Jordan said, pulling Rowan by their hand.

"How were you late already?" I asked. "It's only the first week!"

"Rowan wanted to find a janitor's closet to make out in," Jordan said. "But they're all locked."

"Really? A janitor's closet?" Alex asked, disappointed.

"It's in all the movies!" Rowan said.

I rolled my eyes. "Come on, just use the handicap stall like a normal queer," I said, making everyone laugh. "Or a car."

"Portable privacy," Jordan joked.

"Yeah, but the janitor's closet! It's in all of the One Direction fan fictions I read in middle school. I feel like that would heal my inner child more than years of therapy," Rowan said, dramatically placing a hand over their chest.

"You could just screw one of the members," I offered.

Rowan waved that away. "Nah, they're old now."

"You make me sad," Alex said. She smiled at me and waved goodbye before hurrying down the hallway. I left the couple and went upstairs to my class, trying to figure out how to convince my parents to let me go to the party tonight.

Turned out, my parents didn't care. Hell, Mom even asked if I could stay at a friend's house so I wouldn't bother them coming home late. I didn't know if I should be happy that they trusted me, or upset that they didn't care. Maybe both.

Alex picked me up. "You're sitting shotgun," she said as I waved goodbye to Peter. "Dumb and Dumber are in the backseat. Oh, and I'm not gonna drink, so I can drive back. Please don't overdo anything. I'll be really pissed if we have to take you to the ER for alcohol poisoning. And if you go anywhere private with anyone, let someone know, and text us every half hour so we know you're safe. Oh, and there's this guy, Maxwell. Big white dude that looks like Kianu Reeves if he never hit puberty. Don't go near him, he's a misogynistic asshole on the Tumblr list of unsafe guys."

"Good to know." I said, getting into the car and struggling to process all of that information.

"We need to be safe," Alex said. "We can be safely irresponsible if we plan."

"I love that saying," Rowan said from the backseat. They were sitting sideways, with their feet in Jordan's lap.

"Put your seat belts on!" Alex snapped. "Everyone," she said to me.

I chuckled and fastened my seat belt. "Yes ma'am," I said, mock-saluting her. Alex adjusted her mirrors and checked everything before driving away.

"Alex drives like an eighty-year-old," Jordan said.

"My insurance goes down the safer I drive; I have an app," Alex said. "And I'm broke as hell."

"Do you work?" I asked. "I'm thinking about getting a job, too."

"I work at a Korean-barbecue place. We make rice bowls. Pretty good job," Alex said. "I think the Bookmark is hiring, and maybe the Poodle."

"What's the Bookmark?"

"It's an indie bookstore, really cute," she said. "I think I know someone that works there, or used to work there. I can ask them to get you an interview."

"Don't I have to apply online?"

"Usually, but it's a mom-and-pop," she explained. "Ro, where's the house again?"

As Rowan gave Alex directions, Jordan used the Bluetooth to play what had to be the gayest songs I've ever heard. And not just the camp, Lady Gaga shit, either. It was an eclectic mix of Girl in Red, Conan Grey, David Bowie, Dusty Springfield, Hayley Kiyoko, Queen, Hozier, Towa Bird, Tracy Chapman, Troye Sivan, *Glee* covers, and Lil Nas X. I insisted they send me the playlist, as it was a queer masterpiece.

Once we got there, it was clear as to why Veronica was hosting. The house was fucking huge, and in the middle of nowhere. The cars parked all over the lawn made me glad we were a little late, since we didn't have to navigate the mess.

We all got out and Alex made sure all of our phones worked and we all had access to the group chat. "Check-ins every half hour, just send a text or something. And if you—"

"Come on, Mom," Rowan complained. "You gotta relax a bit."

"I'll relax once I'm asleep," Alex snapped.

"Come on, try the whole self-love stuff. You could do a bunch of stuff to relax. Run, paint, read books, do weed, bake cookies, masturbate—" Rowan's list was cut short by Jordan's hand covering their mouth.

Rowan then licked Jordan's hand, and Jordan wiped it on Rowan's face. "If you wanted to gag me, you could have just asked."

"You're going to hell," Jordan said, getting some hand sanitizer from Alex which she, of course, brought.

"Hey, here for a good time, not a long time," Rowan said. "Now if you'll excuse me, I'm going to go check on the bar. See you bitches later." They jogged off to the house and met up with a couple dudes dressed in all black.

"Fucking emos," Jordan said, rolling their eyes.

"Should we be worried about them drinking too much?" I asked. Alex and Jordan shook their heads.

"Rowan doesn't drink," Jordan said. "They literally only want to see the bar to make fun of whatever alcohol Veronica's parents have, and probably to fuck around making cocktails from Google and Pinterest. I'd be surprised if they don't end up running the damn thing."

"Real cocktails?" I asked. Jordan shrugged. I liked cocktails.

"Not real-grade shit, but yeah. Most people prefer whatever jungle juice is being passed around, like punch or the kegs in the back," Jordan said. "Speaking of the kegs, I'm gonna get some beer. Want any?"

"No thanks, I have to be on my third drink to stomach the taste of beer," I said. Jordan shrugged and went around the back of the house to the kegs.

"Ready?" Alex asked, linking her arm through mine, and we entered the party.

CAT

"Can I have a Fireball and pineapple juice?" I ask the dude with neon-green hair behind the bar. "And, like, seventy-five percent pineapple juice."

"On it, hot stuff," they said with a wink. There were a couple theater kids and burnouts hanging out around the bar, but most people were drinking outside. The bartender handed me my drink, and I immediately downed it.

"Can I have another?" I asked. They looked a little concerned, but made me one. They didn't put as much Fireball in it this time. Whatever.

"You new to parties?" they asked.

I shook my head. "Nope, this is actually my friend's party. She throws them all the time."

"Then why're you so nervous?" I rolled my eyes and hopped off the bar stool. Fuck this.

"I'll be back for more in about an hour," I said, walking away.

"I'll save some pineapple juice for ya, then!"

I found Maddie outside, dancing up against some senior I remember from a yearbook photo of the Spanish club. I think his name was Jaylen. He was pretty hot, for a guy. He was nothing compared to Maddie.

"Whatcha drinking, hon?" Mickey asked as he walked up to and stood beside me.

"Fireball," I answered. Mickey made a face.

"What? Ya still on a whiskey kick?"

"It makes me look cool."

"To who?" I asked. He elbowed me.

"I'm just saying, you should get a cocktail or something fruity. Guys might actually hit on you if they knew you were gay."

"I have bleach-blond hair. I have black painted nails. I wear pearl earrings. I'm in guy-liner. If someone can't tell I like guys, their gaydar is so fucking off."

"You're not in theater or band or a stoner. You should hang out with more of them, so you can try and lose your virginity before we're senior citizens," I joked.

"What makes you think I haven't?"

"You would have told me," I said. Mickey shrugged.

"You told me about that handjob from sophomore year for half an hour. Thirty minutes about how someone touched your dick. Thirty. Minutes."

"You don't tell me when you and Ryan do stuff," Mickey said. "Is he shy? I can totally picture him getting too nervous to get it up."

"None of your business," I said, sipping my drink. "Hey, y'know the name of the guy behind the bar?"

"Oh, that's Rowan. They're in theater, one of the potheads. They're not a dealer, though. But, I think they might sell vapes? They at least help people buy vapes, because they know someone at the gas station." Mickey shrugged. "Not really my type."

"Didn't mean it like that," I said. "Your type is way more Denzel Washington."

"That is such an old reference," Mickey said. "Isn't he, like, seventy?"

"Okay, then. Your type is Micheal B. Jordan. Or, what's his name? The comedian that was in that show about the community college with the gay dean?"

"One, it's called *Community*. How dare you forget the name of one of the most iconic shows ever. Two, his name is Donald Glover, I think. I'm like, eighty-six percent sure," Mickey said. "And yes, those would be better celebrity crushes than a seventy-year-old. What'd I even do with a senior citizen? Get discounts for the movies so they can fall asleep? Drive them to doctor appointments?"

"Whatever, he was hot in that movie with Forest Gump," I said.

"Cat! Come dance with me!" Maddie yelled. I downed my drink and handed the empty cut to Mickey before she took my hand and dragged me onto the floor. I'd read too many Reddit horror stories to ever leave a drink unattended. Even if it's with Mickey, he could put it down and walk away. Better to leave the cup empty or toss the drink.

Maddie was in a really short skirt. I had no clue how she bought it with her dad. Or how she left the house in it. There was no way she snuck past her dad and her three brothers, right?

"Dance with me!" she yelled over the music. Her breath smelled like gin. I rolled my eyes, tried to keep up with her, and failed, miserably. After three songs of me dancing like I didn't know left from right, Maddie turned to me. "It's too loud, wanna go upstairs?"

"Sure," I said, checking my phone. Ryan hadn't texted. I looked around and saw him playing flag football with a few guys and a couple of the girls on weight lifting before following Maddie inside.

We headed upstairs and tried to find an open room to hang out in for a bit. Most were locked. Even the bathroom, from which I heard someone swearing and gasping.

"I'm shaming you!" I yelled through the closed door. "You better not be having sex in someone else's bathroom."

Maddie gasped before grabbing my hand and running away from the door.

"If they come out, I'm blaming you," she said as she pulled me into a dark hallway. We both were laughing so hard we had to use the wall to steady ourselves. Together, we peeked around the corner to make sure the bathroom door was still shut before continuing our search for an open room.

"Found one," Maddie said, once again taking my hand and pulling me into the bedroom. She jumped on the bed and stretched, arching her back and holding her hands above her head, making her already-short crop top completely reveal her bright-red bra.

"What're you looking at?" Maddie asked, following my eyes. "Oh, yeah. I got it at Victoria's Secret in a BOGO deal they had over the summer. Pretty good quality. We should go bra shopping sometime."

"I heard that they have to feel up your chest to get your measurements. Like, they grope them like they're checking for breast cancer." I cringed. "Sorry."

"They don't do that," Maddie said. "They do measure your chest to get a good size, so you need to make sure to be wearing just a tank top or a good bra. I wore a sports bra and got a size too small. I had to return it. They only let me because it was more the worker's fault than mine."

"Who did you go with? I can't imagine your dad taking you."

"Oh. Yeah, I've been helping this girl on the pre-varsity team named Stacy. We went together, over the summer," Maddie said, smiling fondly, in a way I didn't recognize. "She'll definitely be on the varsity team next year. She's a junior, but she was on the varsity team at her old school. The transfer was too late for her to make the varsity team this year, but she's better than most of the juniors on our team."

"That sucks," I said. I don't know why, but my whole body felt like it was on fire. I looked at Maddie again. My eyes fell across her chest and her midriff and her legs. They traced their way up to her hair and lips and eyes. She was beautiful. And I was drunk.

At least that's how I justified it when I leaned forward and kissed her. Maddie put her hand on my neck and pulled me closer, kissing me deeper. She tasted like gin and cranberry juice. Her perfume was vanilla and she smelled like sweat and weed from dancing.

She ran her hands through my hair and pulled me closer, pushing her mouth into mine. I wondered what color my lipstick was now that hers was mixed with it.

Every part of me felt alive. I wanted Maddie's lips on my neck and her hands all over me. I wanted to feel her skin against mine. I'd never felt like this with Ryan. With Ryan, it was boring and uncomfortable. His stubble scratched my cheek and his cologne made my head hurt. Maddie's mouth made me make noises I didn't know I was capable of.

I leaned over her and straddled her lap. I put my hands on her waist before sliding them up her back to unhook her bra. Then, she pushed me off.

"Sorry, sorry," I said, standing up to give her space. My head was reeling, though whether it was the kiss or the alcohol, I couldn't say.

"Fuck, no, I'm sorry," Maddie said. "I'm dating someone."

"Oh, fuck. Shit, I'm so sorry." I didn't know she was dating anyone. Why didn't she tell me?

"Stacy. I'm dating Stacy," Maddie said, as if reading my mind. "And you're dating Ryan. And you're straight. And drunk."

"Yeah," I lied. I could tell her. I felt tears well up in my eyes. I wanted to tell her. "No, I'm not."

"You're not what?" Maddie asked.

"I'm… not straight. I don't like guys," I confessed, looking at anything but her.

"Then, why are you dating Ryan? Does he know?" Maddie said. "Sorry, not helpful." She stood up and hugged me. "Thank you for telling me."

"I'm sorry I kissed you," I cried, hugging her back.

"I wasn't against it," Maddie said. "But we've both been drinking. And I really care about Stacy. In fact, I'll probably tell her about this tomorrow."

"Don't tell her—"

"I won't tell her it was you," Maddie said. "But I trust her and I want her to be able to trust me. God, I'm such a fucking idiot. You know I liked you? Like, back in freshman year."

"I liked you, too," I said. "Damn, if only we lived in fucking California."

"We're still gonna be friends, right? 'Cause you're, like, my best friend and I don't want this to ruin it."

"Yeah, we'll still be friends. We're drunk. It happens," I said, rationalizing it to myself.

She took a step back. "Okay, I'm gonna head home. Do you need a ride? My brother is picking me up."

"No, I'm with Mickey," I said. "I'm gonna stay up here for a bit."

It was too fucking awkward. I wished I was a smoker, so I could dramatically light a cigarette on the windowsill like in a black-and-white French film. That always looked very therapeutic.

"See ya at practice on Monday," Maddie said, closing the door behind her. I scrolled through TikTok for about half an hour before I went downstairs for another drink. After my third, I was finally drunk enough to go and play the perfect girlfriend for Ryan. Little did I know, this would be the last time I could do this.

Because when I woke up on Saturday, I had an anonymous message on Instagram.

everybodyandnobody: if you dont want this posted to the grapevine youll do exactly as I say

Attached was a photo of me and Maddie kissing. I ran to the bathroom and threw up. I couldn't tell if it was from the Fireball or the photo.

ANDI

"What do you think I should drink?" I asked Rowan. According to Alex, they loved this game. They grinned, made a reddish drink, and handed it to me. I took a sip. "Vodka cranberry?"

"Ya like?"

"A little basic, but good."

Alex was leaning with her back against the bar, watching Jordan play beer pong. She smiled as Jordan won and people cheered.

"Once they get a drink in them, they're a complete extrovert," Alex said. "They'll be so embarrassed about this tomorrow. I need to take photos."

So, Alex and I headed outside to record Jordan play beer pong and later hold someone's legs up for a keg stand. We wandered around the backyard for a while after. It was a large field surrounded by row after row of trees. Alex and I climbed and sat in the branches of a small one.

"Hey, Andi, I need to talk to you about something."

"Yeah, what's up?" I asked, turning to her. She was staring straight ahead, her eyes fixed on some flag-football game.

"I'm… ugh, I really hate doing this." Alex took a deep breath before continuing. "I'm trans."

"Oh," I said. "Wait, which way?"

Alex laughed. "I'm a guy," he said. "I just really hate telling people. I don't really wanna announce to everyone that I wish I had a dick, y'know?"

"Sure," I said, even though I didn't really understand. It was hardly my place to judge. "So, do you want me to call you a different name?"

"No," he said. "I'm just Alex. I did go by Lexi for a bit in elementary school, but that was just because there was another Alexandria, and it got confusing. I hate 'Alexandria.' It's such a mouthful."

"'Andrea' makes me sound like I'm in my late thirties," I said. "I sound like a secretary."

"I like Andi, it's cute. Fits you," Alex said. "I don't know when I'm gonna transition. Probably not for a few years. My family's really Catholic. If they found out, I'd be on the streets."

"Damn," I said. "My parents just don't give a shit. Well, they don't want me to tell my extended family that I'm gay 'cause people might think they're bad parents. But nothing aside from that."

"That's messed up," Alex said.

I shrugged. "Not the worst thing they've said by a mile. Or the worst thing strangers have said. You gotta have thick skin to exist. I feel like in response to 'woke, accepting culture,' conservative bigots have just become so much worse with their shit. Like, I got punched in the face by a guy in middle school for telling him I didn't want to go out with him because I had a girlfriend. He got a slap on the wrist and his parents called. When I tell people about it, they act really surprised. Like, that shit really does still happen in the twenty-first century! Just because we got the right to marry doesn't mean that hate crimes don't still exist!"

"That still sucks," Alex said. "Did you hit him back?"

"And risk being seen as an aggressor? Hell no. The school had a no-fighting policy. If I hit back, I would have been expelled," I said. "I just ran away."

"Damn."

"It is what it is." I shrugged. "Wanna come inside with me? I want to get a real drink. Maybe shoot something strong enough to make me wanna dance in public."

"Liquid luck," Alex joked, jumping from the branch. I followed, but lost my footing, fell, and scraped my arm on the roots.

"Ouch! Shit!" I checked my elbow. It stung like hell. "God damn it." The first drops of blood emerged from my torn skin and gathered at my elbow before running down my arm.

"Let's get you inside," Alex said. We made our way inside and headed upstairs to the bathroom. Alex locked the door and helped me sit down on the tub. He went through the medicine cabinet and found some Band-Aids, Neosporin, and some cream I couldn't identify but recognized.

"This is gonna hurt," Alex said, already pouring the hydrogen peroxide over my elbow. I cursed, gritting my teeth. There was a jiggling of the door handle.

"I'm shaming you!" someone called through the door. "You better not be having sex in someone else's bathroom." Alex and I looked at each other for a moment before we both burst out laughing.

"That was hilarious, who has bathroom sex?" I said, drying my tears.

"I don't know," Alex said. "Sex really isn't my thing."

"Never done it," I said.

"I did once with Jordan. I couldn't finish, and then I had a panic attack about going to Hell. Not the best experience." Alex smiled. "So, Jordan helped me put on sweatpants and texted Rowan, and they came over and drove us to this puppy store where you can pet the dogs for free. And then we got ice cream."

"That sounds nice," I said.

"It was," Alex said as he finished applying the Band-Aids. "Okay, I'm gonna text Ro and Jordan and—shit, where's my phone?" Alex asked, feeling his pockets and then searching his purse.

"We should retrace our steps, maybe you left it on the bar and Rowan has it."

Rowan didn't have it, although they did have a new drink for me. Alex and I searched for almost an hour, to no avail. Eventually, Jordan found Alex, and the couple continued to look for his phone while I returned to the bar with Rowan. "One day, I'm gonna be rich enough for my kid to have house parties," I said, feeling the alcohol. I smiled. This was nice. I felt warm and happy, like even my atoms were hugging each other. I could fall into this feeling and I'd trust it would catch me.

"Hey, can I have another?" Cat asked, speaking to Rowan. She looked so pretty. She was wearing a red, plaid dress with spaghetti straps and a slit going up to her mid-thigh.

"Cat!" I stood up, steadying myself on the bar. "You look so pretty."

"Thank you, Andi," Cat said, looking around. "Your… You look—"

I looked at myself. I was in ripped dark-green skinny jeans and a dark-blue tank top. I looked okay.

"Hot," Rowan offered. "You look really fucking hot, Andi."

"Not my words, but yes," Cat said. "You look… gorgeous." She drank the rest of her cup and handed it back to Rowan.

"It's your sixth drink, Cat. Let's get some water in ya before you pass out," Rowan said, handing her a cup of water. "You too, Andi."

"Fuck off," Cat and I said in unison, but we laughed as we hit the red Solo cups together and drank the waters.

"I'm gonna go now," Cat said. "Nice seeing you. Rowan, right?"

"Yeah, I'm Rowan," they said.

"See y'all around," Cat said, stumbling to a guy with bleach-blond hair waiting by the door.

"Another water, please," I said. Rowan smiled, and I drank another water before Alex and Jordan asked if we wanted to leave.

CAT

everbodyandnobody: there is a phone in your locker put it in the lost and found before school

I went pale as I opened my locker on Monday. I'd just come from before-school weight training for cheer and football. There it was, the phone.

Whose was it? Did it matter? Who was messaging me?

I put the phone in my pocket and headed down to the front office with my water bottle. If anyone asked, I'd say I was on my way to fill it up.

The lost and found was a locked filing cabinet in the attendance office. Lucky for me, I was an attendance aid in my junior year, so I knew where the key was.

I placed the phone in the bottom of the drawer, under several vapes, phone chargers, Apple Watches, calculators, and a container of canned cheese.

I exited the office without anyone noticing me. There were only three people in the front office, and they barely looked up from their coffees or computers. It wasn't strange to see me around the school at odd hours. Perks of cheer, I guess.

But how did the blackmailer know that I had access to the office? And what was up with the phone? Who did it belong to? Was this enough to keep me safe?

Once I finished filling up my water, I headed to the showers. I'd long ago gotten over any embarrassment when it came to showering. I stripped and stepped into the shower, where someone, probably Del, had hooked up a Bluetooth speaker and was blasting Little Mix as a pump-up playlist. It worked.

I showered and dried off, putting my hair into two tight braids before pinning them up to create two buns. I changed into blue jeans and a pastel-orange crop top. Our school's dress code prohibited crop tops—and tank tops, for that matter—but that rarely stopped us. The one time I'd been told I needed to cover up, I said I'd had to give my jacket to a friend to hide a blood stain on her pants. The teacher let me go.

I did my makeup in my phone's camera as everyone else in the locker room chatted around me. I saw Maddie talking to a girl—her girlfriend, Stacy.

Stacy was pretty. She had blonde hair with pink ends, which only made her eyes—so dark they were almost black—even more striking. She was wearing sweatpants and a Dolphins Cheer T-shirt. She reminded me of one of my cousins. I could see why Maddie liked her.

I put on my regular, fake pearl earrings and a simple gold chain. I wanted to appear with dignity and class, to command people's respect by showing them that I respected myself. It was something my father taught me when I was young that'd always stuck.

I met Ryan outside the locker room.

"Hey, wanna get breakfast?" he said cheerfully. If Mickey thought I was an early bird, it was only because he'd never seen Ryan in the morning.

"Where?" I asked. "School starts in thirty minutes."

"Treehouse?" he asked as we walked to his car.

I nodded and smiled. "You know my weakness," I said, getting into his passenger seat. "Bacon and caffeine."

"I'm gonna get their meat-lover's bagel sandwich," Ryan said. I grimaced. The sandwich was like if a turducken could be served for breakfast. It was an Asiago and bacon bagel with three egg whites, cheddar, mozzarella, ham, turkey, bacon, and roast beef. It had, like, fifty grams of protein in it.

We talked about classes and senior year as he drove. Once Ryan got our food, we drove back to the school to eat in the senior parking lot. I wanted to kiss him. I wanted to convince myself that kissing Maddie was a mistake, so I could forget it. I wanted to think of Ryan like I did Andi. I wanted to want Ryan like I wanted Maddie.

So I kissed him. He smelled good, like pinewood and citrus. He tasted like his black coffee. I held him by the back of his neck and kissed him deeper, trying to use his lips to erase hers. I could like kissing him. It wasn't bad. It wasn't like my first kiss, with a guy whose name I can't remember, on a dare in freshman year.

The guy had licked his lips before kissing me, and it was far too wet, and he grabbed my chest, so I yelled and shoved him away. Then he told me it was all a joke and that I should have had a better sense of humor. I'd laughed it off, but Mickey punched him in the face for me. I often wondered if he's why guys stayed away from me for years. I was grateful for that.

Ryan and I met in the beginning of junior year. I'd gotten a job at The Treehouse and could get people free coffee, so I had to talk to all the cheerleaders and football players to take their orders. It helped a lot with running for HOCO princess last year; everyone knew the girl who could get you free coffee.

I met him one day when I was trying to carry a bunch of drinks by myself. He pulled up a few parking spots to my left and helped me hold everything. He wasn't a quarterback yet. I wasn't a captain. But we both wanted to be. I think that's why we became friends. His ambition mirrored mine in a way that was reassuringly familiar.

Kissing Ryan wasn't terrible. But it was nothing compared to kissing Maddie. Even though I kissed Ryan like I was trying to suck out his soul through his mouth, even though he gasped at my every touch, it didn't come close to Maddie. Even our brief kiss was better than this.

It wasn't Ryan. It was me. I just didn't like me.

I pulled away as my phone buzzed, leaving Ryan dazed as he adjusted the hoodie sitting in his lap. Mickey had texted me asking to meet outside of the cafeteria.

"Gotta run, see you around," I said, kissing Ryan's cheek before grabbing my food and backpack and heading out to meet Mickey.

###

"Did you see the new article?" Mickey asked as the first-period bell rang.

"What new article?" Did *The Grapevine* post the photo?

"You know Alex Wilson? Apparently, he's a trans guy who has been closeted for years. The writer found years' worth of messages between him and his partner talking about everything: body dysphoria, sexuality, their sex life, their polycule thing, Alex's experience with self-harm. All of it, and now the entire school knows everything."

The phone.

That was hers—no, his. His phone.

I helped *The Grapevine* do this to him. Out him. Ruin his life.

And I was just relieved they didn't out me—that I was safe. I was selfish. But so fucking relieved.

"That's terrible," I said. "What do you need me for?"

"You should interview him about *The Grapevine*."

"Who, Alex?" I asked. Mickey wanted me to interview the outed trans guy? I got enough shit for the Andi interview. I couldn't risk my reputation to interview him. What would people think of me?

"Yeah," Mickey said.

"I'll run it by Livingstone," I promised, knowing full well I wouldn't. What would the article even be about? The impact of coming out? Being outed? And what could I even add to the conversation?

"I'm just saying," Mickey said. "It could help a lot of people. It's an opportunity to help any other trans kids at the school and let them know they're not alone. To let Alex tell his story instead of being forced to accept *The Grapevine's* version. It could focus on the invasion of his privacy. It would be amazing. College application worthy," Mickey bribed. He knew me well, but sadly not well enough.

"I'll think about it," I lied. Mickey smiled and put his arm around my shoulder.

"You're a great friend, y'know that?" Mickey said as he walked me to class. I smiled, but felt my spine shatter. I was such a fucking coward.

ANDI

"Have you seen the article?" Rowan was standing in front of my parking spot, their arms crossed over their chest, looking more pissed than I'd ever seen them.

"What?" I asked, getting out of my car..

"Did you see the article? Did you know? Alex said he told you at the party, and we told him not to, but he said he could trust you—"

"Wait, what happened?" I asked, slinging my backpack over one shoulder as Rowan grabbed my wrist and dragged me to Alex's car. Alex was hunched over, crying in the driver's seat, and Jordan was standing outside the car hugging him.

"Someone found Alex's phone, hacked it, and outed him," Rowan said.

I felt like I'd been doused in cold water. "How much?"

"Everything, stuff I didn't even know about," Rowan said. "Anything Alex would ever want to keep private, the entire fucking school knows."

"My parents texted telling me to come home," Alex said between sobs. "They saw it, I don't know what's gonna happen."

"I'll go with you," I offered. "I can drive."

"They'll probably want the car," Alex said. "They helped pay for it."

"We'll figure that out later," I said.

"I'm driving him," Rowan said as Jordan handed them the keys. "Andi, you should stay."

I wanted to go with them. I wanted to make sure Alex was okay, or at least got to a point where he would be.

"Alex?" I asked, hoping he would ask me to come.

He wiped his face and smiled sadly. "You should stay, hear what people are saying," he said. "You're the only one who wasn't referenced in the article."

"It wasn't me!"

Alex laughed. "I know," he said. "I've seen your writing, it's a miracle you passed English last year. But still, we need someone to know if the school makes an announcement or something happens."

"Okay," I said. "But text me as soon as you're alright, deal? Wait, did you ever find your phone?"

"Yeah," Jordan said. "It was in lost and found. Which is bullshit because he lost it at that fucking party, so how the hell did it end up on campus?"

"This was planned," I concluded. I knew what I had to do. I had to find out who wrote this article and take everything from them. Their friends, their reputation, any morsel of respect anyone had for them. I was going to destroy them.

CAT

All anyone talked about all day was the article. The school was truly divided over it. Some guys misunderstood the post and thought that Alex was a trans woman. They posted a bunch of shit about how if you're born a man, they'll fight you like a man. Dumbasses.

Each grade-level counselor sent out an email about cyberbullying and how if you see something, you should say something. Ms. Rodrick even included a page with mental-health resources like a suicide hotline number and the Trevor Project. I was surprised she knew what that was.

I got a text from Andi in second period.

Andi: did you read the article?
Me: The entire school has. I'm sorry, I heard he was your friend.
Andi: he aint not dead.
Andi: do you know who wrote it?
Me: No, nobody knows.
Andi: you should find out and release their identity in your paper
Me: I'd need major proof for that. They're too smart to give any hints.

Andi: I narrowed it down to someone who was at the party on Friday, who was allowed at school early, and who has access to the lost and found.

How did she know that?

Me: Why?

Andi: Alex lost his phone at the party. There is no way it was at the school unless someone broke in and placed it.

Me: Are you sure? He could have been mistaken

Andi: I was at the party when he entered, and he had his phone. I have a text from him as we entered the party. Then, I was there when he lost it. So, yeah, I'm pretty fucking sure, babe.

Me: You text like you talk

Andi: Thanks?

Andi: You said you'd need proof. If I can get you some, will you write it?

Me: I've been trying to find the writer for years. They're a ghost.

Andi: They destroyed one of my friends life without a second though. I'll burn they're bones if their a ghost. I want them gone.

That was weird to find hot, right?

Me: Meet me in Ms. Livingstone's room at 1:45 after school. We can compare notes.

Andi: Deal.

What was I getting myself into?

ANDI

"Did you read it?"

"Of course, can you believe it?"

"So, is it a dude or a chick? Like, really?"

"Why didn't they come out?"

"I heard it killed itself."

"I think it's really brave for him to come out."

"I heard her parents are gonna get in trouble with the pastor about raising something… like that."

I clenched my fists as I walked to my third period trig class. I wanted to scream and yell and punch all of these transphobic assholes. I hadn't read the article. If Alex wanted me to know something, he could tell me on his own.

Then, just my luck, I ran straight into a girl while walking to class. In my defense, she was wearing earbuds, texting, and walked into me.

"Watch where you're going," she snapped, brushing off her shirt as if I spilled something on her.

I rolled my eyes. "You walked into me, but okay," I said, stepping around her.

"You're that chick's friend, right? Alexandra?" she asked.

"His name is Alex, and yes, he is my friend," I said through gritted teeth.

"Sorry, didn't know you were a democrat," she said, laughing. "Well, please send her my prayers. It's gotta be so embarrassing, right? And her family is so religious, imagine them hearing about the trans thing? And the suicide attempt, and the sex stuff? God, I'd be so humiliated."

"What the fuck is wrong with you?" I said. Screw this. "Do you get off on being a prick? Seriously, is this some kind of kinky thing where you get off on talking shit about people? I mean, fucking really? It's not 'embarrassing' because Alex did nothing wrong. You can't shame someone who was in the right."

At this point, people had started to gather 'round. I should have stopped, but I saw the fear in her eyes and wanted to go in for the kill. I thought back to last year and how I didn't stand up for myself. How I walked the halls, ashamed and scared of what people were saying. I would never be that girl again.

"I'm embarrassed for the author! They probably won't do anything better in their entire life than write shit about random teenagers on a blog all of two-hundred people read. And, I feel bad for you. It must be so embarrassing, having nothing in life besides what your parents have given you. It must be so embarrassing, having to shit-talk strangers to feel in control of your life. Do you feel big? Does this make you feel good about your pathetic excuse for a life?"

I heard the slap before I felt it. The bitch slapped me across the face. It wasn't even a punch. As if I was beneath her, as if she didn't think I could take a hit. I glared at her and hooked my glasses to the front of my shirt before raising my fists. I knew how to fucking fight, and I was fine proving it if she needed a demonstration—

"Lisa!" a teacher yelled. "Did you just slap her?"

"I didn't—"

"She did," someone said. It was the blond guy Cat was with at the party. "She slapped her."

"You're just taking her side 'cause you're both gay," Lisa accused.

The blond guy shrugged. "How does that even work? I've never even met her," he said. "And we have security cameras to confirm it."

"She was calling me a bunch of names!" Lisa cried. "It was verbal assault!"

"You hit her," the teacher said. "Principal's office, now. All three of you."

Lisa looked like she wanted to protest, but turned and huffed down the hallway ahead of us.

"I'm Mickey, by the way," the blond guy said. "You're Andi, right?"

"Yeah," I said. "Thanks for defending me."

"You were in the right. And she was being a bitch," Mickey said. "Don't worry, they'll just make you fill out a report saying what she did, and then they'll send you back to class."

"You've been in my shoes before?" I asked.

Mickey shook his head. "No, I've just witnessed it a few times. Track kids don't get into a lot of fights," he said. "I'm gonna go to college on a scholarship, can't fuck that shit up."

"Felt that," I said. "I wanna go too, can't risk anything on my record."

"You'll be fine, at least you didn't hit her back." He opened the door to the front office. "My lady," he teased, and I fake-bowed before stepping inside. For the first time that day, I smiled.

CAT

Andi looked as amazing as ever. She was in dark-purple jeans and a lavender crop top embroidered with flowers.

"Hi, Cat," Andi said, moving to sit on top of the desk next to where I was standing. She was shorter than me, but like this, we were almost the same height. "So, notes?"

"Yeah," I said, withdrawing my journal and last year's yearbook from my bag. "Can you go through and see who you recognize from the party?" I asked as I handed her the yearbook.

"Can I write in it?" Andi asked, and I nodded. She pulled a Sharpie out of her back pocket, uncapped it, and started circling a few names in the yearbook.

"So far, I have it down to seniors who are on sports teams," I said.

"And someone who would have access to the front office," Andi pointed out. "Someone who wouldn't be noticed."

I should have told her about everything. The messages, the phone, that I helped *The Grapevine* author, even on accident. But I was too scared, so I kept my mouth shut.

I didn't want Andi to hate me. I didn't know what I'd do if she did. Being near her made everything else go quiet, even just for a moment. I existed only in a singular moment in her presence. She was like an anchor. I didn't know what I'd do if I had to face the current alone.

"Can I work with you on this?" Andi asked after a few minutes.

"What?" I asked.

"On finding the author," Andi said, smiling. "We can find proof against her and tell everyone! It's the perfect revenge!"

"It's more than just revenge, it's years of stuff. Of her controlling what everyone thinks. If she used her platform to help people, it would be different, but she uses it like a weapon. And she's good at it."

Over the years, the author had written several articles about queer kids, speculating on details of their sex lives. It was revolting. The only good article she ever wrote was on a girls' weightlifting coach who was sending nudes to his students. When I first read it, I was excited. I thought the author had changed and was going to do real work now, proper journalism. The next week's article accused a student of cheating on her ex-boyfriend because she was seen with a male friend the day after they broke up.

I think that's what I was angry about the most. *The Grapevine* had so much power and potential, and they chose to use it to hurt others instead of uplift them.

"You could be better," Andi said. "I read some old articles you wrote. You're a better writer than her, especially when you're reporting on something. Like that piece you did last year about that Mexican restaurant that got shut down for breaking child labor laws. That was good shit."

"Thanks," I said, blushing. Mickey had been so happy when I released that, but almost everyone else thought it was too political and opinionated. I hadn't published an article like it since.

"No problem, babe," Andi said. "I gotta go, I need to call Alex."

"I'm sorry about all of this," I said. "It must be terrifying." I would be terrified, if all my secrets were out there, for the entire school to see.

"Yeah," Andi sighed. "Rowan's been texting me to let me know that they're okay, but I haven't heard from him since before lunch."

"Let me know if you need anything," I said. "Even if it's just someone to talk to."

"Thanks," Andi said, jumping off the table. "I circled everyone I remembered from the party."

"I'll cross-reference it," I said. "See ya tomorrow."

"See ya, babe," Andi said as she walked away.

—

I was distracted at practice.

Between the blackmail and the article and Andi, there was no way I couldn't be. And having Maddie there, acting like nothing happened… It was too much.

"Hey, I'm gonna head to the bathroom," I tell Coach. "Ronnie, can you cover for me as Mads's spotter?"

"On it," Veronica said, giving me a thumbs-up. I grabbed my phone and left. I just leaned against a sink for a bit and scrolled through Pinterest. I didn't want to be out there.

That's when I heard the scream.

I don't remember leaving the bathroom. Maddie was on the track, and her ankle was bent the wrong way. I could see a little bit of white bone before it was covered by blood, flowing out onto the black concrete.

There was too much blood. Why was there that much blood? I felt like my bones were made of stone. Every movement I made felt like it was in slow motion. I suppose I never could have been fast enough; I never would have been able to prevent Maddie from bleeding out on the track in the first place.

"Call 911!" I heard Coach yell to Veronica.

"What should I do?" I shouted at Coach.

"Pressure," she said, tossing me a clean towel. I wrapped it around Maddie's ankle as she screamed through gritted teeth. I don't know how long Stacy had been there, but she was kneeling on the ground, holding Maddie's hand.

"The ambulance is gonna be here soon," Coach said. "Maddie, I need to call your dad."

Maddie took out her phone and handed it to Coach. She looked confused, so Stacy took the phone, unlocked it, called Maddie's dad, and handed the phone back to her.

Stacy and I stayed next to Maddie until the ambulance came. I was covered in her blood, staining my hands and leggings a dull red. So was Stacy.

I felt like someone had shot caffeine straight into my veins. I'd never been so angry in my entire life.

Veronica was supposed to be fucking spotting her. I turned and walked across the field toward her. "What the fuck happened?" I snapped. I didn't recognize my voice. I was so fucking scared, and now all that emotion turned into pure, fucking rage.

"I'm sorry, I thought she was fine—"

"What part of your training as a spotter told you to let her fall?" I screamed. "You don't fucking think, you just do!" Lisa started, "Maybe if you stayed—"

"Shut the fuck up," I said. "Maddie is hurt—"

"Is she dating that blonde girl?" Miracle asked. "I didn't know that was allowed."

"That has nothing to do with—"

"Green!" Coach said. She spoke with a commanding, steely calm. "Go home."

"What? You're benching me?" I asked.

"No," Coach said. "But you need to go shower and… clean up. Go home, relax."

"I'm fine—"

"That wasn't a request, unless you want me to bench you. Go home."

I glared at her but grabbed my backpack and stormed off of the field.

ANDI

"So, is this your first job?" Mrs. Johnson asked as we sat down in her office.

"No," I said. "I used to work as a cashier in Tampa. My boss wrote me a letter of recommendation, I included it in my resume."

"Oh, yes, I see now," Mrs. Johnson said. "So, why should I hire you?"

"You should hire me because I learn from my mistakes," I said. "Will I be perfect? No. But I can promise you that I will never make the same mistake twice. I will always show up to work at least five minutes early, I'll always show up prepared, and I want to be here. This isn't just a job, it's something I enjoy."

"What's your favorite book?" Mrs. Johnson asked. I smiled as I thought.

"It depends, but right now it's *Last Night at The Telegraph Club* by Malinda Lo," I said. "Or *When the Moon Was Ours* by Anna-Marie McLemore."

"Have you ever read *Ash*? It's also by Malinda Lo," Mrs. Johnson said. I smiled and shook my head.

"I'll get you a copy before you leave—for free, of course. And I'll get a sheet with your training schedule written down. You'll get two Bookmark T-shirts, one blue and one red. It'll be forty dollars off of your first paycheck. You saw that it's only twelve dollars an hour, right?"

"Yes ma'am," I said. "Thank you so much."

"You're welcome. I'm taking a chance on you, Andrea. Don't make me regret it." Mrs. Johnson said.

"Oh, it's Andi, actually. That's what everyone calls me." I said. Mrs. Johnson nodded and corrected the sheet she had for the interview.

"What pronouns do you use?" Mrs. Johnson asked. I'd never had an adult ask me that.

"She/her," I said. "And it's Andi with an I."

"But there are no I's in your name," Mrs. Johnson said, clearly confused.

"Yeah, it's a Peggy-Margaret thing." I shrugged. Mrs. Johnson looked as if she wanted to ask something, but stopped herself.

I followed her out of her back office and into the front of the store, and she handed me a copy of *Ash*. "I'll make your schedule, one moment," she said, leaving me at the cash register. That's where I saw Cat.

She looked… hollow. She was wearing plaid pajama-bottoms and her wet hair hung out of her black hoodie.

"Cat?" I asked, causing her to jump.

"Hey, Andi," Cat said. "Shit, I look terrible, I normally look better than this."

"Are you okay?"

"I… I got sent home early from cheer practice." She swallowed. "My friend broke her ankle. It was really bad and now I'm here. I went home and showered and went to read a book, but Mickey had it, and if I wanted to get it back I'd have to explain why I'm home early, and then he'd want to do something to get my mind off of it and talk about it and—"

"What book?" I asked. She smiled and handed it to me. It was *Simon vs The Homosapien's Agenda* by Becky Albertalli."Great book," I said, handing it back to her. "Have you seen the movie?"

"Yeah," she said. "I like the book better."

That meant she was gay, right? Like, what straight girl reads Becky Albertalli?

"Hey, I've read that book, it's really good," Cat said, pointing to the book I was holding. She's read Malinda Lo. Definitely gay.

Fuck it. "Wanna get coffee?" I asked, nodding to The Treehouse that was across the parking lot.

"Can't," Cat said. "Sorry, I told my dad that I'd be home."

"Then, sometime?" I asked. "Maybe we can go out and—"

"Andi, here's your schedule," Mrs. Johnson said. "Oh, I see you've met Cat. She's a regular here, I'm sure you two will see a lot of each other."

"We go to school together," Cat smiled, handing Mrs. Johnson the book. She was smiling again and was standing up straighter. Every ounce of vulnerability and sadness had been erased from her face, as if it'd never even been there. I never noticed how much of this was a performance until I saw behind the curtains. I liked the real Cat better.

"Haven't you already bought this?" Mrs. Johnson asked as she rang it up.

“Yeah, but a friend’s borrowing it permanently,” Cat said. “What can I say, it’s a comfort read.” Cat picked up the book and smiled at me. "See you around, Andi," she said as she walked out of the store.

“So, here is your schedule. I made sure not to do anything on Friday nights,” Mrs. Johnson said. “You’ll only be working twenty hours a week. This isn’t a law, but it’s a rule here for high schoolers.”

As she explained the rest of my schedule, I watched Cat walk to her car and look back over her shoulder. We locked eyes before her face went red and she drove away.

CAT

"So, here is the list," Andi said, sliding me a folded piece of paper. We were in my room. She'd asked to come over to discuss *The Grapevine* author, and I'd stupidly agreed.

It was late, around 8 p.m. Cheer practice had ended a bit ago. It was terrible. Lisa and I bickered back and forth all day, and Miracle was a jerk to Stacy. Well, the entire team was. Nobody would talk to her. I didn't know if it was because she was dating Maddie or because she replaced her. Probably both.

"What's this?" I asked as I unfolded the paper. I knew all the names on it.

"It's everyone who had access to the school over the weekend and on Monday morning and could have put the phone in the locker," Andi said.

Fuck. I needed to tell her.

"It was me," I said, looking away. "I put the phone in the office, but I swear, I didn't write the article."

The color drained from Andi's face. "Why?" She asked, her voice unsteady.

"I need you to swear to never tell anyone," I said. Andi nodded. I got out my phone and showed her the messages from *everybodandnobody.*

"Are you and her together?" Andi asked. I shook my head.

"I have a boyfriend, and she has a girlfriend," I said, looking away. I felt like I was gonna throw up. "But I… I don't like Ryan, not like that. I don't like guys."

"Then why are you dating him?"

"If people find out about this, about me—you see how people have been over me writing that article about you. We're not in California. Sure, we have a couple liberal teachers. But you've seen it. The most we get is a safe-space sticker on a door, or a get-to-know you sheet asking for preferred names or pronouns. And that's the exception, not the expectation.

"Hell, the gym coach still calls people 'fruitcake' and 'fairy.' I've heard people get called fags so often at practice with football I'm not even fazed anymore. I've gotten where I am through my reputation. If I'm no longer seen as the perfect girl, I lose all of it."

I got up and paced as Andi stayed seated on my desk, her emerald eyes tracking me like a cat. It felt natural to tell her everything. It had been so long since I was honest I had almost forgotten how good it felt. I told her because I thought she'd understand. And at the very least, I trusted her not to tell anyone.

"Why don't you write about this? Call out the football players and coaches and gym teachers," Andi said. "You could change—"

"Nothing, Andi. I can't change anything," I said. "Listen, I'm sorry I put the phone in the office, and I'm sorry I lied. I regret it. I just wanted to show you why I did it. I didn't have a choice."

"You always have a choice," she said. "But your actions really didn't affect shit. The article still would have been posted. The phone would have just been in your locker instead. But, you should have fucking told me yesterday. If we're going to work together, you can't lie. About anything. Ever."

"I won't," I said, and I meant it. I never wanted to lie to her again. If she was choosing to give me her trust, I wasn't going to be stupid enough to break it.

Andi nodded and took the paper. "This list still applies, because someone had to go to your locker in the first place. Who knows the combination? Wait, fuck. If the author is using blackmail, then they could have gotten someone else to put it in your locker."

"My cheer team knows my locker combo," I said. "I sent it to the group chat when I wasn't there and someone needed pads. Ryan knows, so does Mickey."

"Anyone else?" Andi asked.

"If someone could get into the front office, attendance has a sheet with everyone's locker numbers."

"They probably couldn't get into the office, that's why they needed you. So, it has to be someone who knew you had access to the office," Andi said.

"That could be anyone, I wasn't secretive about it."

"This is why privacy is important," she mumbled. "So, the cheer team. Varsity or pre-varsity?"

"Both," I said. "I can get you a list of everyone who attended that practice, and we can work our way from there."

"Wait, I'll only need seniors because the party was seniors only," Andi said. "And then I'll ask Alex about who he recognizes."

"How is he?" I asked. "I didn't see him in school. I have some work for him." I had a class with Alex, and they handed out a study guide for the first test. I asked for a copy for him, which I now handed to Andi.

"That's really nice, babe," she said as she put it in her backpack. She looked up at me through her eyelashes. Her smile was breathtaking. What did I need to do to see that smile every day? Whatever it was, I'd do it.

"No problem," I said. "Um, anyway, you were saying? About Alex?" *Words, Cat, they are something that exists for communication. You've known how to use them your entire life, don't forget now.*

"Yeah, he's staying at Rowan's house. He turns eighteen in October, and his parents kicked him out. We're going over tomorrow while they're at church to get his documents and everything. They didn't really give him time to pack up his shit."

"That's terrible," I said.

Andi nodded. "He's doing better than I'd be. Can I see the list again?" I handed it to her, and she highlighted Lisa's name. "She's a dick, it could be her."

"I'll work on it," I said. "Yeah, she's a dick."

"We got into a fight on Monday, I kinda roasted her ass and then she slapped me. Oh, your friend, Mickey, helped me not get in trouble. He's cool."

"Yeah, he is. But she hit you?" I asked. Andi nodded. Why was she still on the team if she assaulted a student?

"It's whatever. Won't be the first or the last time I get hit," Andi said with an indifferent shrug. "What, you've never been in a fight?"

"No, why would I?" I asked. "That's really unusual."

"Depends on where you're from," she said with a smirk. Her phone buzzed and she groaned. "Ugh, Peter wants me to come home."

"Peter?"

"Little brother," Andi said as she grabbed her purse. "If he texts that he wants me home, I have to go."

"Okay," I said, getting up with her. "I'll walk you out."

Andi followed me downstairs and to the front door. "Thanks for having me over," she said.

"Thanks for coming." I didn't know what to do with my hands. She looked just as awkward as me. Then, I hugged her.

She was still for a moment, but she hugged me back. She smelled like coconut and lavender and some third thing that I couldn't quite place but knew was very sweet.

"Thanks again," she said as we pulled away. How long did the hug last? She hurried out the door and I watched her drive away before locking the door.

"Someone's down bad," Hannah said from behind me, making me jump.

"What did you say?" I asked, my pulse in my throat.

"Nothing," she said, walking away.

ANDI

Rowan's foster parents lived in the middle of nowhere. It was almost an hour from my house.

Their house was two stories, with a large backyard that was fenced in for their dogs. Rowan's foster dad had painted the outside light purple—their foster mom's favorite color—for her birthday a few years back.

"Hey," Rowan said as I pulled up. They were pacing the driveway, vaping.

"Your parents know you put that shit in your body?" I asked as I locked my car.

"Yes, and it could be worse," Rowan said, putting it in their pocket. "I could be drinking or doing weed."

"Instead, just a hit of metal to the lungs, got it."

They rolled their eyes and flicked me off. "Here for a good time, not a long time, Andi," Rowan said. "Alex is inside. He looks a little different from Monday."

I nodded and headed inside. Alex had insisted I not see him till Wednesday, when I was finally allowed over. I'd never been to Rowan's house before, so they showed me to the guest room.

Alex's room was bare. The bedsheets were plain white, and the walls were naked. Everything looked so… boring. Alex and Jordan were on the bed, watching TV.

Rowan was right. Alex did look different.

In the last two days, he had cut his hair—which was now short and faded from the nape of his neck to a little longer on the top—and apparently co-opted Jordan's wardrobe. Instead of his typical, modest clothing, he was wearing men's gym shorts and a wifebeater that revealed his binder. In total, he looked more comfortable than I'd ever seen him.

"Hey, looking good, man," I said to Alex once he noticed me.

"Thanks," he said, getting up. "I figured, screw it, right?"

"Yeah, screw it. Hey, Jordan," I said, nodding to them. They nodded back and smiled, looking at Alex. I wondered if anyone had ever looked at me like that. Like I was their entire world.

"Okay, ready to go break into my parents' house?" Alex asked, grabbing his purse and pulling out a pair of house keys.

I grinned. "Fuck yeah."

Getting into the house was pretty easy. The key still worked, and Alex disabled the security system quickly. The hard part was finding the safe with his birth certificate.

"Can someone else check my parents' bedroom?" Alex groaned. "If I find a sex toy or condoms or something, I'm killing myself."

"Cute! We should do it together, be all romantic and shit," Rowan called from Alex's dad's office. "We can even leave a note, Ram-and-Kurt style."

"They were murdered, they didn't commit suicide," Jordan corrected. "Y'all would be like Romeo and Juliet."

"I call dibs on Juliet," Rowan said. "Remember when I played Paris? That was cool."

"You're the only person that likes Paris," Alex said.

"I don't like him," Rowan said. "But I liked playing him."

"Whatever," Alex said.

I was looking in the guest room. After a few minutes, I found the safe. It was in an Amazon box in the closet. "Found it!" I yelled. Alex came running and unlocked it.

"Jackpot!" he said.

Then, we heard the front door open.

"Shit," Alex whispered.

"Alex's room, go," Rowan said. The four of us tiptoed upstairs to Alex's room, listening to his family bring in groceries.

"I swear I locked the door, David," Alex's mom said. "We should check the doorbell camera."

"I recognized that car parked down the street," David answered. "Don't you?"

Jordan closed Alex's bedroom's door and locked it. They pulled out a couple garbage bags from their pocket. "Start throwing shit in."

As quickly and quietly as possible, I filled my bag with jeans and hoodies and shirts and socks and underwear and anything that would fit. Jordan carefully unlocked the bedroom window and dropped the bag out gently onto the soft grass below.

We were silent as we waited to see if anyone heard. We did this till we had filled up three bags. Alex collected anything important to him. I watched as he left family photos in favor of yearbooks and novels. He grabbed his jewelry, put his laptop in a pillowcase, and tried to gently lower the bag out the window.

"I'll go first." Jordan lowered themselves slowly from the windowsill, keeping hold of it and landing on their feet. "Ro, your next."

Rowan did the same, although not as gracefully. I didn't know how I could do that. I wasn't as slim and fit as Jordan and Rowan. I probably weighed fifty pounds more. Alex made it look easy, too, although I realized it was probably a skill he'd gained through practice.

"Andi, your turn," Alex whispered. I tried my best. I lowered my legs so that half of me was hanging off of the windowsill and half of me was on. Then the gutter broke off, which did wonders for my body image.

The good news was that I landed on a bag of clothes. The bad news was that Alex's family definitely heard that.

"Run!" Jordan yelled, grabbing two bags and hauling ass to the car. Alex and Rowan grabbed bags and followed them, but I wasn't fast. I was dressed in black skinny jeans like an idiot.

"I'll text y'all where I am!" I yelled as David came out of the house. "Hey, dumbass!" I taunted him and ran down the street in the opposite direction.

David was far bigger than me and looked to be in his sixties. He'd run after me, but I'd probably beat him on pure fear and adrenaline.

I zigged and zagged through the suburban cookie-cutters until I saw a familiar house. David was a block behind me, and he would keep chasing me if I didn't hide. So, I took a risk. I ducked around the side of the house, opened the fence, and went into the backyard.

"Andi?" I heard someone ask. I turned around to see…

"Cat?" I asked. "Shh, be quiet!"

Cat looked over the fence to see David charging down the road and past the house, yelling something about calling the cops.

"What did you do?" Cat asked. She had her hands resting on her hips and was dressed in a white, two-piece bathing suit. Her hair was down, tangled at her shoulders.

"You have a belly-button ring?"

"Why is he talking about the cops?" Cat asked. "Oh, is that Alex's dad?"

"Smart," I said. "I didn't know you had a pool."

"I do. Come over here, it's only Mickey and me," she said, taking my hand in hers and leading me into her backyard proper from where I'd been hiding on the side of the house. Sure enough, Mickey was there, tanning on a laid-out beach chair.

"This is Andi," Cat said. "But I've heard you two already met."

"Yep," Mickey said. "You want a piña colada? Virgin, of course."

"Sure," I said. Mickey got up, went to an outdoor patio bar, and poured me a piña colada from a Margaritaville blender. "Thanks," I said, taking a sip. It actually was non-alcoholic. I was kinda surprised.

"Why was he chasing you?" Cat asked. "Are you okay?" She wrapped a lace robe around herself. It was black and see-through. Her silhouette in the white bathing suit against the black lace was very distracting.

"Um—sorry, what?" I asked, feeling my face heat up as I looked away from her.

"Why was he chasing you?" Mickey asked.

"Oh, we broke into his house to get Alex's clothes and papers, since he was kicked out," I said.

"Fuck," Cat said. "That's shitty."

"Did you get caught?" Mickey asked.

"He could try and call the cops," I said, repeating what Rowan's foster dad had told us. "But he'd have to explain why he kicked out his seventeen-year-old kid and was keeping his documents and passport, and that would make him look like shit in court." Just then, my phone went off.

"Where are you?" Rowan yelled as I answered the call from Alex.

"Are you okay?" Jordan asked.

"Did you get caught?" Alex asked.

"I'm at Cat's house, I'm okay, and I did not get caught," I answered.

"Is he gone? Do you want us to come get you?" Jordan asked. "Ro's circling the neighborhood."

"Hey, Cat, can I stay here for a bit?" I asked. She nodded. "Nah, I'm good. Y'all should get home in case he's still out there."

"Okay, but you text us every half hour, okay? And let us know when you get home, and—"

"God, stop being such a dad, Alex," Rowan groaned. "Don't do anything I'd do, Andi. Bye!" With that, Rowan hung up.

"I'll give you a ride home in a bit," Cat said. "I'm just gonna shower to get the chlorine out of my hair."

"Me too," Mickey said. "Not at the same time, I just also need to shower." He turned to me. "I'm so gay I make Elton John look as straight as John Cena."

"Okay," I said. "Kinda figured, with the hair and all. Plus, you sound like Kurt from *Glee*."

"Which season?" he asked.

"Season one."

"Fuck, he sounds the gayest then," Mickey said. "Really? Don't think I could pass?"

"As straight? No. As a drag queen? Probably," I joked, making both of them laugh. Cat headed inside. I watched her leave. She looked stunning.

"Speaking of straight," Mickey said. "You ain't got a chance, hon. You're barking up the wrong tree with her. She's Quinn Fabray. You're Santana. Not gonna happen."

"Well, they did have sex, canonically."

"Bad example," he said, waving it off. "She's Fabray and you're… Dani!"

"Who?"

"That other girl Santana dated after Brittany, when she lived in New York."

"I have a feeling I'm in over my head with your talking about *Glee*."

"You'd be right, I watch it annually," Mickey said. "Anyway, you should chase after someone who might actually be gay. Or is gay. Like Rowan, they're nice."

"Not my type, and dating someone," I said.

"You should join theater, you could join a harem there."

"I'm pretty sure the politically correct term is a polycule," I said sarcastically. "Not really my thing."

"You ever date?" Mickey asked.

I shrugged and took a sip of my drink. "Never been on a real date," I said. "I used to see this girl, last year… She was in the closet. Didn't want anyone to know. And then we got caught making out in a bathroom during lunch, and she said I made her do it. Fucking ruined me. She said she was going to press charges, but I had messages from her proving that she had agreed to it. Still, she told everyone that I forced her, so even though I was proven innocent, the lie stuck. My parents jumped at the opportunity to move here."

I hated talking about her. I hated even thinking about her. I remembered trying to deny the allegations and nobody believing me. I went through every interaction she and I had, trying to see if I misread the signs. She'd kissed me first, almost every time. She had texted me first, making plans to fool around.

I knew I hadn't done anything wrong. But a small, sad, part of me was glad people believed her. I knew how shitty it felt for something to happen to you and for nobody to believe you. I knew how it felt to be at the other end of their disbelief, and I would never wish that on another woman. But, of course, in this case, people believed her lies. They were nicer than the truth. That she had wanted me. That she had begged for me. And I'd been stupid enough to say yes, so of course *I* was the deviant.

"Damn," Mickey said.

"So, I understand why I can't like someone like Cat," I said. "I don't fuck with straight girls. I only date girls who are out."

"I had a thing with a guy once," Mickey said. "Didn't last very long. He was just experimenting."

"Here's to the tragedy of falling for straight people," I said, and Mickey and I clinked our glasses together.

"Hey, Andi," Cat called. She was wearing light-blue, silk pajama shorts that showed off her long, tan legs and a white, almost see-through, silk button-up pajama blouse. "I can drive you home now."

"Yep," I said. "Yep. Yeah, sounds good."

"Stay strong," Mickey whispered as I handed him my drink. "You can do this."

"I'm doomed," I said as Cat turned and walked away.

"You're doomed," Mickey agreed, and I trailed after her like a lovesick puppy.

CAT

I was scrolling on my phone in the library when Andi kicked my legs off of the ottoman and sat on it.

"What're you doing?" she asked. She was in ripped blue jeans, a matching blue tank top, and an unbuttoned black overshirt that was too large on her.

"Looking at different colleges," I answered. "You wanna go to college?"

"Yeah," Andi said. "Don't really know what for yet. I'll probably apply under communication or marketing or something. What do you wanna do, babe? You seem like the type with goals and shit. Do you have a college-themes Pinterest board?" she teased, smiling.

"Yes, I have 'goals and shit'," I said in air quotes. I pushed my hair over my shoulder. "I'm gonna go into journalism."

"What would you do with that? Like, I've seen *Anchorman*, but—"

"I want to be an investigative journalist," I said. "Think more like Courteney Cox's character from *Scream*."

"Oh, I liked her in those. She's hot as the bitch character." Andi nodded.

I looked around. Hardly anyone was here. It was second period, and I'd gotten permission to come up and read in the library because I finished my assignment yesterday and the class was too loud to read in.

"Yeah, she's great in those," I said. "I like the new main character, Billy Lomis's kid?"

"Oh my god, she's amazing in those," Andi said. "I heard a bunch of people hated her 'cause they thought it was too cliche, but I love the darkness she has. Like, she can seriously fuck someone up."

"What're you doing up here?" I asked.

Andi shrugged. "Got bored in class," she said. "Saw you in here and decided to bother you."

"Well, thanks. It's made my day a lot better." I smiled. Was that flirting? I was flirting, right?

"My pleasure, babe," Andi said, smirking back. Okay, she was definitely flirting. "Oh, I was wondering when you could do the interview for Alex."

Shit. Yeah. That. I regretted giving Mickey her number.

"I'm gonna be really busy with cheer practice because of the football game this Friday," I said, looking away.

"Come on, Cat," Andi said. "He's available anytime. Hell, you could write down the questions and I could ask him."

"I just—I don't want him to get more negative attention," I said. "What if this just pisses more people off?"

"He's already getting bullied. He's had to delete all of his social media accounts and change lockers. At least this way he gets the last word."

"But what if *The Grapevine* posts something else in retaliation?" I asked. *What if they post something about me?*

I had seen Alex in class today. He looked okay, but every few minutes he would just stare off into space, as if he wasn't in his own body.

I imagined myself in his shoes. It very well could have been. It could still be, one day. If it were me, I'd want people to hear my side of the story. I'd want to get the last word. But *The Grapevine* still had my photo. I didn't know if it was worth the risk.

"Come on, he can take it. What else could they possibly say about him?" Andi asked. The bell to end second period rang and Andi stood up, grabbing her book bag. "This could help other trans kids, other queer students. Come on, Cat."

"I just—I don't know," I said, still avoiding her eyes. Andi was looking at me quizzically, like she knew something was off. She stepped closer to me. She smelled like lavender and coffee.

"If this is about the Insta—"

"It is. If they post it—"

"What if I write it?" Andi asked. I shook my head. "Come on, it needs to be done."

"I'll write it," I said quickly. If Andi wrote it, *The Grapevine* might post something about her, and she would get all the shit Alex was. I wouldn't let it happen. I'd rather take the heat myself then let her get caught in it. If she got hurt by any of this, I'd never forgive myself.

"If you're sure," Andi said.

"I am," I said, nodding. I noticed she had on a glittery eye shadow along with her typical thick black eyeliner. "Your eyes, they look cool. I like your makeup."

"Thanks," Andi said, blushing and taking a step back. "See ya 'round, babe," she said as she walked away. I put my book in my bag and looked up to see her looking at me over her shoulder. She blushed again and hurried away.

ANDI

The article came out on Wednesday. It perfectly framed *The Grapevine's* piece as a terrifying invasion of privacy, and ended by criticizing *The Grapevine's* clear abuse of power in ruining a random student's life without anyone caring.

Cat's name was not on the article. In fact, it officially had no author, although I wondered who else had recognized her writing. She wrote like she spoke when she was excited.

Me: badass article

Cat: It has no author.

Me: thank you for writing it. It means a lot. Wanna get ice scream after school? my treat to celebrate the article

Cat: Sounds good. Send me the address and I'll meet you there.

The entire day passed by quickly, me just waiting to go out with Cat.

Maybe I had a crush on Cat. She was kind and sweet and funny and beautiful. She was so confident and self-assured. And for some reason, she liked my company. If that's all she ever wanted from me, I'd spend my entire life letting her enjoy it.

I dropped off Peter at the house and then drove to the Poodle. Cat had said she'd be a bit late too, because she had to drop off Mickey, so we ended up arriving at the same time.

"Are you out to him?" I asked as we read the menu.

"No," Cat said. "I know he'd be fine with it. He's gay, and he loves me. It's just—I don't want anything to change yet. And I don't want him to think I don't trust him 'cause I told you and Maddie before him."

"Well, it's not like you really told Maddie. More so shoved it down her throat," I said, prompting Cat to elbow me. "Abuse!"

"Shut up," Cat laughed. "I'm gonna get the mint–chocolate-chip."

"So you like your toothpaste frozen?" I teased.

She rolled her eyes. "It's good! It's not too sweet and has just the right amount of chocolate. What're you gonna get that's so much better?" she said, crossing her arms over her chest.

"I will be getting the peanut-butter–chocolate-chip–cookie-dough ice cream," I said. "It's limited edition."

"Do you get the limited edition all the time? Like, is that your regular?"

"Well, I've only been here twice, but yeah. If it's limited edition, it's usually really good," I explained. "I've only not liked one limited edition thing, which was a peach lemonade at a fair. And that was only 'cause they had peach skins in the lemonade."

"Oh my god," Cat laughed as we ordered our food. She handed the cashier a twenty-dollar bill that she pulled out of thin air as I reached for my card.

"I said I could pay," I said as we waited for our ice cream.

"I'm sure you could have," Cat said.

"I have a job now. I have adult money but no bills."

"Twelve dollars an hour is not adult money," she stated matter-of-factly. "The minimum wage is bullshit and not realistic for adults."

"Agreed. But you know what I mean."

"There will be other stuff you can pay for."

"Umm, Cat, I've been meaning to ask, what's up with you and the boyfriend?" I asked, immediately regretting it when Cat grimaced.

"It's complicated," she said as the cashier handed us our cones.

"We have time," I said as we walked over to the bench I'd sat at with Rowan, Jordan and Alex three weeks ago.

Cat pulled her hair into a low ponytail to stop the wind from whipping it around. I pulled up my hood. She looked over her shoulder, making sure the lot was empty. She'd once told me she was an open book. I was going to test that. I wanted to know everything there was to know about her, anything she would tell me.

"I just… *The Grapevine* had just posted this article where I was really close to Maddie. It was a loud crowd and she was trying to ask for a tampon, but that didn't matter. So, the article supposed that I liked girls. But only a few people really believed it. And then Ryan asked me out and I thought it would be a good idea to go to prom with him to get people off my back. But then I just didn't know how to dump him. And he's so sweet and kind. I just thought that maybe if *I tried* hard enough, I could like him; I could take all these thoughts and feelings and put them in a box and replace them with what I was *supposed* to feel. But then—it didn't work," Cat said. "I should break up with him soon, though. He deserves to be with someone who cares about him like he wants them to."

"You could explain it to him like you did to me," I said, desperately resisting the urge to take Cat's hand. "I'm sure if he's like you say he is, he'll understand."

"I'm sure he would," she chuckled. "Which just makes it harder. He'd be happy for me to come out, and he'd be all nice and supportive and shit."

"Can I be honest with you?" I asked. Cat nodded and bit into her cone. "It seems like you're getting in your own way with coming out. I get that it's not easy, but you have a good group of friends that'll be here for you."

"I've worked too hard in cheer to have it become a thing I hate," Cat said. "I know their support shouldn't matter, but it does. I want to have that place where I can just be around my teammates without them thinking I like them or that I'm looking at them in the locker room."

"Is it really a safe place if you can't come out? If you can't be yourself?" I asked. "If you're paranoid and having to hide parts of yourself, is it really that great a place to begin with?" I knew how paranoia could eat at someone like a vulture. It would tear you apart. I didn't want that for her.

"Maybe not," Cat conceded. "But it's mine."

We ate in silence. Eventually, I asked, "So, you wanna stay in Florida?"

"For college, at least. Out-of-state tuition is a bitch. After, I wanna move to New York."

"I love New York," I said. "There're just so many people that it creates so much privacy, you know?"

"Yeah," she said. "And there's always something to do."

"I guess there isn't a lot to do down here," I said. "Would you miss anything? The weather, the hurricanes, the oranges?"

"No," Cat laughed. "I actually don't like oranges."

"What? Oh my god, you're a serial killer, right? First the mint–chocolate-chip ice cream, now this?" I said dramatically, and Cat dissolved into giggles.

"They're just so sour, and the texture is weird! Plus, sometimes you get a bit of the white part and it's bitter and gross. And way too much stuff is orange flavored: orange soda, orange popsicles, orange muffins, orange cake. It's just too much!"

"I didn't know you were so passionate about this," I said, smiling. "You're cute when you get excited."

"Flirt." Cat blushed. We talked and finished our ice cream before heading to our cars. "It was great hanging out with you," she said.

I pulled her into a hug before she turned away. She was so warm. I usually didn't like hugs, but with her, I felt safe. Less like she was grabbing me and more like she was holding me. Like I was something precious and delicate.

"I liked hanging out with you too," I said. I wanted to tell her that she should dump her boyfriend so I could take her on real dates and hold her hands and kiss her and—

She pulled away, but her eyes stayed fixed on my lips. I thought she was going to kiss me. In that moment, it didn't matter that she had a boyfriend, or that I swore to myself to only date girls who are out. The only thing that mattered was that I needed her lips on mine like I needed air. I needed to know how her ChapStick tasted, how her hair felt when I ran my hands through it.

"See ya, Andi," she said, walking away.

"Good night, babe," I called as I got into my car. I needed to either get over her or talk to her. This crush was going to be the death of me.

Cat was going to be the death of me.

CAT

I spent the rest of the night narrowing down the list of potential authors to the varsity cheer team and the football team. I realized that although the author didn't have to be at the school for them to put the phone in the office, they did have to put it in my locker. All I needed to do was get the security tapes.

Which I knew how to do.

On Thursday, I went to school early to work out in the weight room with the other cheerleaders. It was pretty easy to get out. I said I was sick and was going to get some pain meds from my car for cramps.

Instead of going to my car, I walked into the front office and into the attendance office again. Thankfully, nobody was there.

A small part of me felt bad abusing Mrs. Rodrick's trust to log into her computer and pull up the security-camera footage. I remembered the date and searched the main atrium camera from Friday night to Monday morning.

That's when I saw her. "Miracle?" I stared at the black-and-white footage incredulously. It was definitely her.

A familiar heel-click echoed from down the hallway, approaching the door. I pressed the power button on the computer and hid under the desk as the door opened.

"Hey! Mrs. Rodrick? I've been meaning to ask you, I have a free period during fifth, can I leave campus?"

Mrs. Rodrick started talking, and I heard her take a few steps away from the door. I looked through the window to see Mrs. Rodrick talking to—Miracle? What was she doing here?

I opened the door slowly and stepped out. Mrs. Rodrick didn't notice. She was deaf in her left ear, which was facing the door. Did Miracle know this, or was it a coincidence?

I left through the front office and went back around to the gym. Miracle wasn't there. It had been her. So why was she helping me? Why didn't she let me get caught? And why had she had the phone?

ANDI

My shift was only four hours. Mrs. Johnson—or Marie, as she asked me to call her—was on shift too. Today, I was in charge of dusting and organizing the shelves.

As I wandered through the store, I realized how much I liked doing this. I loved the Bookmark. I liked the records Marie kept of every purchase and order and sale. It made sense.

"Marie," I said once I got back to the register. "How did you open up the store?"

"It was a lot of licenses," Marie said, putting down the book she was reading. It was something written by Taylor Jenkin Reid. "And I'd saved up for almost ten years after college. I used my husband's GI Bill to get my degree in entrepreneurship. And then I worked at other, bigger bookstores and got promoted to manager to learn how everything worked. And then I got a loan and opened up the Bookmark."

"You can get a degree in entrepreneurship?" I asked.

"Yeah," Marie said. "I really enjoyed college. Then again, I didn't go when I was eighteen. I worked as a waitress after I graduated high school and lived with my parents until I got married. My husband was in the Navy, and after he retired, we moved here. He works at Mayport now, as a civilian."

"I feel like everyone expects me to know exactly what I want to do right now," I confided. "But I just don't. I have a bunch of ideas for stuff that I think would be cool, but it's not exactly related."

"What ideas do you have?"

"I saw some TikToks online of hair stylists, and that's cool. But I think my parents would lose their minds if I told them," I laughed.

"Do you do your own hair?"

"Yeah," I said, running my fingers through my bangs. I cut it last weekend, so it was a little above my shoulders, and I had choppy bangs. The red was fading out to a pinkish color, and my roots were growing in black. I was going to re-dye it, but Cat had complimented it, so I wanted to let it stay for a few more weeks. Plus, my hair would probably appreciate a break from bleach.

"It looks good," Marie said. "You could try to be a hair stylist, and if you don't like it, change. You're young, Andi. I know eighteen might seem mature and grown-up, and you are, but you still have enough time to decide. I wouldn't be nervous about not knowing what you want to do yet. At least you have some ideas."

"I also think being a flight attendant would be cool," I said. "Being able to travel all of the time."

"I know someone whose sister is a flight attendant," Marie said. "I can give her your number if you'd like to talk to her."

"Really? That'd be the coolest thing ever," I said, smiling wide. "Thank you."

"No problem, hon," she said. "Can you go in the back and grab the box of signed copies so we can set up the stand before closing?"

"Yeah, on it," I said, and I hurried to get the box for her. Talking to Marie felt so natural, I often forgot we were at work.

My family wasn't like her. My mom and dad really only cared about how amazing I made them look. If I went to college, they would look like great parents. Successful parents.

If I became a hair stylist, they'd think they failed. And they'd take it out on me. I remember when I told them I wanted to join the art club; they asked if it was just to show I was a well-rounded student on college applications. I made the mistake of telling them that I really liked drawing and painting. Maybe I could be an art teacher one day. They asked to see my sketchpad. I'd thought they really wanted to see my work.

Instead, they picked apart every detail of my drawings. They told me it was a waste of time to join the art club, as it wouldn't help me. Art club was for artists, not me. I threw away that sketchpad. I still regretted that. But I was thirteen and dramatic.

After that, I never told them about what I liked or didn't like. And they complained about how they didn't know me and how I was such a typical, moody teenager. It was better this way. I didn't get hurt as much.

After my conversation with Marie, I decided to do some research into it. I was an adult, I could become a hair stylist if I wanted to. At the end of the day, my parents wouldn't have to deal with me in my late thirties, hating a career I chose when I was eighteen. I would.

It was my life, and my choice. I smiled at the thought as I brought the books out to Marie. It was my life.

CAT

"Hey, Cat," Ryan said as he sat down on the bench. I asked to meet up with him after practice. I figured the park would be a good place. Public, but also quiet enough that we could talk.

"Hey, Ryan," I said, not getting up to greet him like I normally would. "I need to talk to you about something."

"Yeah, what's up?" he asked. He looked excited. Happy. I hated this.

"We should see other people," I said, cringing at the cliché.

"What? Did I do something?" Ryan asked. "I'll fix it, I swear—"

"It's me, not you," I said, because apparently, I was playing cliché-break-up-line bingo.

"Really? 'It's not you, it's me?' That's what you're going with?"

"It's true," I said. "I'm sorry."

"Is there someone else?" Ryan asked. I felt my face redden as I thought of Andi and how close I was to kissing her when we got ice cream at The Poodle. And how I'd kissed Maddie. "Oh my god, there is. You're cheating on me?"

"I'm not," I said. "But—"

"Oh my god."

"I kissed someone," I said. "And I'm sorry, I was drunk and—"

"We can move past this!" Ryan said. "We can work on this—"

"She was a girl," I said, tears welling up in my eyes. Waves of shame rolled over me like a tide. "I kissed her, and I realized I don't like guys. I'm a lesbian."

It felt strange, saying it out loud. The words felt odd on my tongue. Or maybe it was the honesty. This was probably the most vulnerable I'd ever been with Ryan our entire relationship. I really had been a shitty girlfriend. I silently swore that if we stayed friends, I would be a better friend to him then I was a girlfriend.

"Oh," Ryan said. "You should have just said that."

"You can't tell anyone," I begged, wiping my eyes. "Please, I can't—"

"I won't," Ryan said. "I mean, I thought you were bi."

"What?" I asked.

"Yeah, I mean, I thought you and Maddie were something at one point, the way you looked at her junior year," Ryan said with a shrug.

"And that didn't bother you?"

"I'd be a hypocrite if it did."

"What?" *He's gay?*

"I swing both ways," Ryan said casually. "I've only been with one guy, and he said he didn't want anything serious, so I've never needed to come out. But yeah, I just figured you were bi."

"And you didn't say anything?"

"I didn't think I needed to. So, you're a lesbian?"

"Yeah," I said. "I'm a lesbian. I'm sorry."

"No, you're fine, don't apologize," he said. "So, why did you date me in the first place?"

"I thought I just hadn't met the right guy yet," I said. "But you're the greatest. I thought if I could like anyone, I could like you. And you asked me out right after *The Grapevine* posted that article about me, so I said yes."

"Okay," he said, clearly thinking about something. "Do you want to not tell anyone we're broken up?"

"What?" I asked. That was an option?

"I mean, if you dated me so nobody would know you were gay. We can still pretend to date, or just not publicly say we've broken up. We weren't really big into PDA in the first place," Ryan suggested.

"But then everyone would think we're together. You wouldn't get the homecoming experience with a real date, or anything like that," I said. "Why?"

"Even if I date someone this year, we're going to break up when I go to college. So, it might just be easier to be off the market. And I'd like to explore other sides of myself, and it'd be easier to do that if everyone thinks I have a girlfriend. Like, of course I wasn't flirting with that guy, I have an amazing girlfriend," Ryan said, grinning.

"Are you sure?"

"One-hundred percent," he nodded. "And if the girl you have a crush on—"

"I didn't say anything about a girl—"

"—ever wants to actually date you in public and shit, let me know. I can mean-mug the shit out of anyone who looks at you twice," Ryan said.

"You're a Golden Retriever, that'd only work on people who have never met you. I've seen you slam on the breaks for a duck."

"I couldn't hit it!" Ryan argued, causing both of us to laugh.

Ryan and I spent the next hour or so talking about how we knew we were gay and movie-star crushes. It was nice to be treated like how I felt was normal.

Now, I just needed to tell Mickey.

ANDI

"Go Jordan!" Rowan screamed. I covered my ears and glared at them as they leaned over the railing.

Jordan was a part of the school's color guard. They performed with our marching band at football games and were split into 2 teams. There was the flag team—which twirled, tossed, and spun flags while running between band members—and the rifle team, which only used flags when they weren't carrying fake rifles or swords.

Jordan was doing a solo now. The band was rushing around them as they ran on stage doing cool rifle flips and tossing it into the air. I didn't know a lot about color guard, but it looked really fucking cool.

"What's up with their costumes?" I shouted to Alex over the crowd and the band.

"They're supposed to be dolls," he said. The color guard was dressed in checkered, skin-tight leggings and long-sleeve shirts. Most of them had a skirt attached to their leggings.

"The band does a theme each year for shows. This year, it's something about a puppet master," Rowan said. "Also, don't let Jordan catch you calling them costumes. They are uniforms."

"They're kinda touchy about that," Alex explained. "Don't got a clue why, though."

My phone buzzed in my pocket.

Cat: Meet me in the bathroom.

Cat: ASAP

I grinned at the text. "I gotta go to the bathroom," I said once Jordan's solo ended. I hurried away through the crowd before either could question it.

The outdoor bathroom was a hotbox. It was humid and smelled like sweat and weed. Personally, I didn't mind the smell of weed that much, but combined with the sweat, it was disgusting.

"Hey," Cat said once I entered. She was leaning against a sink. "I got a lead on the author, a big one."

"Who?" I asked. "Also, not to objectify you, but damn," I said, looking her up and down. "I've never seen you in your uniform."

She was wearing a small, teal-blue skirt and a lighter top, cut like a vest, with a white tank top underneath. She was in white Converse and her hair was pulled back into two braids over her shoulders. She had on hot-red lipstick, light-blue eye shadow, and twin eyeliner with glitter on her eyelids and cheeks.

"Thanks." Cat blushed. "You look nice too."

"Not as good as you do, babe." I looked okay. I was in ripped, black skinny jeans and a dark-red crop top with a baggy, green hoodie over it. "Sorry, you were saying about the author?"

"Yeah. I found who put the phone in my locker," Cat said just as the door opened. I turned to see another cheerleader. She had dark-brown skin and her braids were cut short around her sharp jawline.

“Hey, Miracle,” Cat said, standing up straighter and schooling her face into a peaceful, indifferent expression. “Can I help you?”

“I was wondering if we could talk,” Miracle asked, looking at me with disdain. “In private.”

Oh. This was her. The author.

“Is this—" I started to ask, but Cat lightly kicked the back of my leg.

“You’re going to the Treehouse after this, right, Andi?” Cat asked. I nodded. “I’ll see ya there,” she dismissed.

I clenched my jaw, annoyed, but left the bathroom.

CAT

The Treehouse on Friday night was the most popular spot in town. They turned on their outdoor lights and karaoke machine, and they usually had a fire pit outside.

Everyone from school knew that after the football game, you went to The Treehouse. You'd get coffee and donuts and someone would DoorDash pizza and you'd eat it in your tailgate in the parking lot while watching a classmate destroy a popular pop song in a sugar-high attempt at karaoke.

I drove Mickey, Hannah, Maddie, and Stacy to the Treehouse. Maddie wasn't allowed to perform with us until her ankle healed. She hated her cast, but at least she'd gotten a lot of signatures.

"If you put on a sad song, I'm pulling a *Lady Bird*." Maddie said as I handed Mickey the phone. He flicked her off.

"Pull a *Lady Bird*?" Hannah asked. She wasn't usually with us, but her mom and my dad were on a date and they didn't want her home alone.

"Tuck and roll out of a moving car," Stacy explained. "You've never seen that movie? It has Timothée Chalamet in it."

"Never," Hannah said. I tuned them out and focused on driving through the stop-and-go traffic. I was still in my cheer outfit and makeup; I didn't really care enough to wash it off. Plus, Andi seemed to really like it.

Once we got there, we headed over to where Ryan, Lisa, Veronica, and a few other football players and cheerleaders had gotten a couple tables.

"That's my cue," Mickey said as his friend, Aiden, waved him over to where track was sitting together.

"I'm gonna get a hot cocoa," Hannah said.

"Hey, you better keep your phone on!" I called as she walked away. I sat down with my friends and tried not to check my phone as I looked around for Andi. I wanted to tell her about what happened with Miracle.

After Andi left the bathroom, Miracle turned to me. "I didn't write the article," she said the second the door clicked shut.

"What were you doing with his phone?" I asked.

"I had to," Miracle said, looking around. "I got this message on Instagram from this person, *everybodyand—*"

"*—nobody,*" I finished. "I got one too."

Miracle nodded. "Then you know the power they have over me," she pleaded. "I put his phone in the locker, but I didn't write the article. Or post it. I don't know who did."

"What do they have on you?" I asked. "If I know, I can narrow it down."

"Don't you see? If you out the author, she'll release everything. On everyone. If my parents find out what I did, I'll be destroyed," she said.

"I'll show you mine if you show me yours," I said. Miracle looked unsure. "Mutually assured destruction."

"Safest way," Miracle relented, handing me her phone. It was open to her messages. I handed her mine.

There was a photo of her with some boy, clearly shot from a window. It showed her back, completely bare. She was sleeping with some guy.

"My family's Baptist," Miracle said as she returned my phone. "If they knew I was having premarital sex, I'd be an outcast. Hell, if they knew I had condoms, or that I've taken Plan B before, they'd have a heart attack."

"Well, I don't want anyone to know about my photo, either."

Miracle nodded. "Are you cheating on Ryan with her?"

I shook my head. "We're not together. Me and Maddie, or me and Ryan," I said. "He and I talked, we're just friends. But don't tell anyone."

She nodded. "Let me know if you find the author," Miracle said. "I'd like to have a chance to prepare before you do whatever you're planning on."

"How do you know I'm planning on something?"

"Cat, I've known you since middle school," she said. "I know when you're gonna go after something. You have that look in your eye. I know you'll find them, too."

"I blame them for Maddie getting hurt," I whispered shamefully. "If I hadn't been so distracted, I would have been there."

"It wasn't your fault. You can't hold on to that guilt."

"I should have told someone when I got the message," I said. "Maybe I could have—"

"Regret does nothing for you," she said. "It just keeps you in the past."

"You can be really poetic, Miracle," I said, and we laughed.

"We do need to go out before the third quarter starts," Miracle said, checking her reflection in the mirror. "Also, that photo doesn't change anything between us, okay? You're still my teammate, no matter whose team you play for." She smiled and held out her arms. I let myself be pulled into her embrace and smiled.

"Same with you," I said. "Who was that guy anyways?"

"You know the linebacker, Jaylen?" Miracle said with a smile. "We've been on and off again since freshman year."

"Really?" I said. "Who would have known where you were? And who knows about you two?"

"I don't know," Miracle said. "The photo was taken over the summer. It was from a beach trip we went on with some friends."

"I need a list of everyone on the trip."

She nodded. "I'll get it to you by tomorrow morning."

"Miracle! Cat! Come on!" Del said, popping her head into the bathroom. "Stop your gossiping!"

"Sorry!" We shared a look and a smile as we hurried out of the bathroom.

I was still looking around The Treehouse when Ryan tapped my shoulder.

"What?" I asked.

"Your phone buzzed," he said, handing me my phone from off the table. It was Andi.

Andi: bathroom. Now.

"So, Andi?" he said as I grinned at the phone.

"None of your business," I said as I grabbed my purse and excused myself.

"I will interrogate you about this later," he called after me, making me laugh.

ANDI

I waited in the bathroom for Cat. It was a one-room bathroom, so I made sure to keep the door unlocked. After what felt like forever, she entered. The only thing that had changed about her was that her hair was down and falling over her shoulders and chest.

"What happened with Miracle?" I asked, hopping to sit on the sink. She closed the bathroom door and leaned against it.

"It wasn't her," Cat said.

"How do you know? If you saw her put it in the locker—"

"She was blackmailed," Cat explained. "By the same person on Instagram who messaged me."

"This is bullshit," I said. "Did this get us anywhere?"

"Closer," Cat said, nodding. "The photo that Miracle had against her had to have been taken on a vacation, so she's gonna send me a list of everyone who was on the trip."

"Great," I said. "And then what? Any leads?"

"We'll figure it out," Cat said. "I think I'm gonna talk to Mickey about it this weekend. He's got friends on the robotics team, one of them has got to be a hacker."

"Cool, fucking great," I snapped. I was pissed at the thought that this person might get away with it. I was pissed that Cat was standing on the other side of the room. I was just pissed.

"You don't have to be in a shit mood," Cat said. "What's gotten up your ass?"

"What is this?" I asked, regretting it the second I said it. "I mean, I just... I thought you were going to kiss me at The Poodle."

"I did, too," she whispered.

"I won't be some... mistress," I said. "If I'll always just be some secret affair while you go on dates with your boyfriend—"

"I told him," Cat said. "I told him I'm a lesbian and we're over."

"Oh." I said, shocked. "Why?"

"It felt wrong," she exhaled, taking a step forward and closer to me. So close that her hands were now just above my knees. "Thinking about you like I do while dating him."

"And how exactly do you think about me, Cat?" I breathed, tilting my head so my hair went over one shoulder.

"Andi, you're the most beautiful, funny, kind, woman I've ever met. I just really love being around you," Cat said, still moving forward. Her hands moved up from my knees, to my thighs, to my hips. I felt like my skin was on fire and her touch was the only thing that could calm it.

"So what? You just really want my company? There's nothing else you want?" I asked, feeling reckless.

"No," Cat said. "I want a lot more than that."

Which, of course, was when the bathroom door opened. Thank god it was Alex. "Oh, sorry," he said, turning and closing the door behind him. Cat pulled back so fast I might have imagined her between my legs in the first place.

"Fuck," Cat swore. "He won't tell, right?"

"No, Alex is really pro-outing people," I said sarcastically as I got off of the sink and brushed myself off. "I'm going to go."

I didn't know if I was more upset that she literally just confirmed that she was ashamed of me, or that I didn't care as long as she kept looking at me like she had before. Like I was some Pandora's box she couldn't help but open.

"Yeah, that works," Cat said, her face flushed. She appeared to be very interested in the bathroom tile. I rolled my eyes and walked out.

Alex, Jordan, and Rowan had gotten seats next to the karaoke machine, and Rowan was doing a surprisingly good cover of *Mr. Brightside.*

"They read a book that started with a quote from the song, and now it's gonna be their personality for a couple weeks," Alex said as I sat down.

"Hey, about the bathroom—"

"I didn't see anything," Alex said, but he smiled as he sipped his coffee.

"You order like a cis-het guy, you know that, right?" Jordan said. "Do you even like dark roast?"

"It's okay," Alex said with a shrug. "I'm trying not to stay up too late on a sugar high."

"So, the logical thing was to order coffee," I explained sarcastically to Jordan. "Oh, wait, is it decaf?"

"Yes, it is," Alex said, rolling his eyes at my horrified expression.

"Oh my god, you're a sociopath. Do you know who drinks decaf? Caffeine addicts and serial killers, Alex. You have the coffee taste of serial killers," I teased, taking a sip of my own hot cocoa and matcha mix.

"Hey!" Rowan said as they sat down across from Jordan and proceeded to use them as a leg-rest. "So, who wants to do a group act?"

"No," we chorused. But of course, almost an hour later, we were up there trying to sing *Don't Stop Believing*. We ended up laughing too hard to do the last chorus and ran off stage before the end, our arms around each other.

CAT

"Why do you hate me?" Mickey rolled over and buried his face in a pillow as I turned on the lights. He crashed at my house last night after we played Call of Duty for a few hours.

"I have practice every Saturday," I said, stepping out of my sweatpants and into my leggings. "And it's seven a.m., not five."

"It's seven a.m. on a Saturday," Mickey groaned. "It might as well be two a.m."

"You have issues."

"They make me funny."

"You're good to walk home whenever you wake up?" I asked as I grabbed my purse. Mickey mumbled what I assumed was a yes before I headed downstairs. Hannah and her mom were in the kitchen cooking breakfast. Ginger followed me out of my room. I was pretty sure I accidentally locked him in my room last night. He likes to sleep under my bed.

"Hey, where are you off to?" Eleanor, my stepmom, asked as she flipped a pancake.

"Cheer practice." I grabbed a Tupperware container and threw in a few sausage patties and pancakes. "I'll be back at three."

"That's so long," Hannah complained. "Is Mickey still upstairs?"

"Yeah," I said. "Kick him out if y'all want."

"He's fine," Eleanor said. "Cat, it's been a while since I've seen that boyfriend of yours. Where has he been?"

"We broke up," I said, grabbing my keys from the rack next to the door. "See ya!"

"We're talking about this later!" Hannah said as I swung the door closed.

I loved Saturday practices. The school was usually empty. The band left for competitions early, and they were on the other side of the school from the gym. Sometimes theater was there, but they were on the stage. Football was out on the field, and softball was in their pitch on the other side of campus. Everyone was far enough away that they all thought they had the school to themselves.

So it was a surprise to me when I saw Andi, Alex, Jordan, and Rowan sitting outside of the school eating out of a donut box.

I should have kissed Andi last night. I wanted to. Neither of us had texted the other. Maybe I fucked it up.

I grabbed the Tupperware and downed a pancake before putting the lid on and heading out to the gym. I tried to keep my head down, but I heard Andi call my name. I tried to play it cool. "Hey," I said, waving.

"Guys, this is Cat," Andi said as she waved me over.

"Want a donut?" Alex looked at me and grinned as he lifted the donut box. My face went red as I thought about him walking in on me and Andi last night. At least we weren't actually making out.

"Thanks," I said as I grabbed a blueberry one. Andi nodded at my pick approvingly. "What're y'all doing here?"

"You gotta sit if you're gonna talk to us," Rowan said. "If not, it looks weird." They had a point, so I sat down next to Andi before Rowan continued, "I have rehearsals for *The Tempest*, and Jor's got a band comp. They're on break, and our teacher hasn't gotten here yet for theater."

"Are you in the play?" I asked Andi. "I remember you said you were in the class."

"No," Andi said. "I'm the person who opens and closes the curtain. I get to wear all black and be emo and shit."

"Should be easy for you then," I joked. Andi nodded as she took a bite out of her lemon-meringue donut. I wondered what it would taste like if I kissed her now. How the icing on her lips would be transferred to mine.

"I'm Ferdinand," Rowan said. "Alex does tech, too."

"You do lights, right?" I asked, remembering that from our interview. He nodded.

"Yeah, this show was so cool with lights," Alex said. "We get to do one of those scenes where the stage lights up in different shapes to show magic. It's really cool."

"Can you send me the dates?" I said, turning to Andi. "I'd love to see the play."

"Are you a Shakespeare fan?" Rowan asked as Andi pulled out her phone.

"Not really," I said. "I'm more into TV dramas with a lot of seasons."

"You ever watch *Supernatural*?" Jordan asked.

I shook my head. "What is it?"

"*Scooby-Doo* for adults," Jordan said. "Oh, it's like, major blasphemy or whatever the term is. It's about two really hot monster-hunter brothers and they fight monsters and demons and angels and gods and literally anything that's not human."

"Sounds cool," I said. "I've been rewatching the *X-Men* movies recently 'cause I can't find cool shows."

"Which *X-Men* films?" Rowan asked, crossing their arms. I felt very much like I was being tested.

"The ones with the hot Charles Xavier," I said, forgetting the actors name. "I think his name's James or something. And the guy that plays Erik is the guy from *Assassin's Creed."*

"You've seen that?" Andi asked. "Do you play *Assassin's Creed*?"

"Yeah," I said. "I got really into those games with Mickey."

"I liked the one with the ships when I was in middle school," Andi said. "My PS3 is still boxed up from the move back in June. I need to take it out."

"Yeah, maybe I can come over sometime and play with you," I said. My phone buzzed. "Shit, it's my alarm for practice. Well, thank y'all for the donuts. See ya, Andi."

"Good luck, babe!" Andi said. "Text me when you're done?"

"Yeah," I said, smiling as I got up and hurried to the door. Coach Roe pulled up in her truck and started walking to the gym. I always tried to get there first.

"Why were you hanging out with them?" Lisa asked as she approached me. "Doing another pity-party article?"

"No, Lisa," I said. I really wished Maddie was here so she could tell Lisa to fuck off.

"Then why? Trying to win the gay vote for homecoming queen?" Veronica asked, snickering.

"Don't tell me they turned you, did they? I knew it, that new girl, it's a thing. She's got her claws in you, literally," Lisa laughed. My face went red as I noticed Andi looking over at me. I didn't want her to see how much of a coward I was.

"You two can shut the fuck up about them, okay?" I snapped. "I don't make fun of your friends, so you can take your opinions and shove them—"

"Oh, they're your friends now?" Lisa interrupted. "I knew Maddie was a fucking dyke, acting like a goddamn embarrassment with that bitch she calls her girlfriend—"

"Lisa!" Coach Roe said. "What did you just say?"

"Nothing," Lisa said, looking down.

"No, what did you just say? Come on, I want to hear it," Coach Roe said. "Veronica, Miracle, Cat, did you hear what she said?"

I could say it. I could tell Coach what Lisa said. She'd be benched or made to run laps. It's not the first time she's said stuff like this, either. But if I did, I'd put a target on my own back.

"I didn't hear anything," I lied. Coach Roe knew it, too, judging by the look of disappointment on her face.

"Well, whatever it was, it sounded like gossip. If I hear it again, all of you will be running laps until I feel like going home, understood?" Coach Roe said. We nodded. "Great, now, get inside. We have a lot to do today."

"Thanks for not being a snitch," Veronica whispered as we walked in.

"What do you mean? I just didn't hear anything." I walked away, wishing I could go sit outside the school with Andi and her friends instead of being at practice.

ANDI

Cat texted and asked if I could come over Saturday night after she was done with practice. I didn't even try to play it cool; as soon as she asked, I texted back yes.

I got to her doorstep as soon as I could, feeling like a girl from a country song. Do you like me? *Check Yes or No.*

"Hey!" Cat said as she opened the door. As soon as I saw her, I was done for. She was in the same satin pajama set I'd seen her in last week. She was clearly just out of a shower and her hair was still wet. "Wanna head upstairs?"

"Yeah." I followed her to her bedroom. Nobody else seemed to be in the house. "Where are your parents?"

"Oh, yeah, they went out to dinner with my little sister," Cat said. She invited me over when her parents weren't home.

"Okay," I said, suddenly feeling very nervous. What did she want? Was she expecting us to have sex? Did I need shots for that? Had she ever had sex? I'd never, though not for lack of desire. I'd just never met anyone who I really thought I wanted to do that with.

"I wanted to talk about Friday," Cat said as she sat down on her bed. Her eyelashes were really long because of the water. Or were they always that long?

"Yeah, what about?" I asked, resisting the urge to pace. I sat down beside her and tried not to twirl my rings on my fingers.

"I really like you, Andi," Cat said, turning to face me. She was staring at my lips. "But I don't know what you want. I can't come out right now—"

I kissed her. I didn't know what I wanted our relationship to be, but I wanted to kiss her so bad. She smelled like vanilla and coconut shampoo. Her lips tasted like strawberry, which was so essentially Cat, I almost laughed. She sat on my lap with her legs on both sides of my hips. She was probably used to making out with a guy.

She ran her fingers through my hair and her nails scraped my scalp. She moved impossibly closer, all of her chest pressed against me and her mouth on mine as if she was trying to do reverse CPR and take my breath away. It was working.

I broke from the kiss for air and she moved her hands up my shirt to my abdomen. "Can I take it off?" she asked, breathless in my ear.

"No," I said, and she removed her hands. "Sorry, I—"

"You don't have to apologize for saying no," Cat said. "Are you okay?" She leaned back and moved so she was beside me.

I nodded. "I don't want to be an experiment," I said. "I won't."

"You're not," Cat said, cupping my face in her hand. "I really like you."

"What does that mean? You want to go on dates?" I laughed. "Or you just want to make out in bathrooms?"

"I don't know, I just need time to come out."

"You don't need to force yourself to," I said, falling backwards onto the bed. "We can just be friends."

"I really liked kissing you," Cat said as she lay down beside me. I turned over to face her.

"I liked that too," I said. "So, we're just friends who occasionally make out?"

"Is that what you want?" Cat said. No, it wasn't what I wanted. I wanted to live in California, or hell, even Tampa so I could hold her hand and kiss her at school and ask her to homecoming. But she didn't want to come out yet, and I couldn't make her. I wouldn't make her. So, I nodded.

"Yeah, it's what I want," I lied. She sealed the deal with a kiss.

CAT

"Wanna go out?" Hannah asked as she opened my bedroom door. I groaned and looked at the time.

"It's eight a.m.," I said. "On a Sunday."

"Good observation," Hannah said. "I'm bored."

"Go on a walk."

"Come on," Hannah said. "We can go to the mall or to the Bookmark. I heard that girl, Andi, works there. Maybe you two can run into one another."

"She doesn't work today," I said, smiling at the thought of Andi in her uniform. "Anyway, what does that mean?"

"Nothing," Hannah said. "Unless there's something you want to tell me. Like, anything you wanna come out and say." Of fucking course she knew.

Hannah and I had lived together since I was seven and she was five. She was a sophomore at school, on the basketball team because she was five-eleven. Technically, she was my stepsister, but I tried not to lead with that. I didn't see the point in most contexts.

"Give me twenty minutes to get ready and I'll take you out. We can go get Waffle House or something for breakfast," I said. Hannah smiled and hurried out of the room. "Close the door!" I called after her, but she was gone.

I closed the door and changed out of my pajamas and into shorts and a button-up. I really didn't feel like putting any work into how I looked, so I braided my hair down my back before I grabbed my purse. Hannah was already downstairs by the time I was ready. She was dressed in jeans, a hoodie, and boots. "Why?" I asked. "You know it's September, right? Not January?"

"I know," Hannah said. "I'm cold."

"It's ninety degrees outside," I said. "Plus, humidity."

’ "It was ninety-five yesterday," Hannah said, proving nothing. I rolled my eyes and grabbed the car keys as we headed outside. "So, wanna play some Girl in Red? Or maybe some Japanese House? Or some Reneé Rapp? Boygenius?"

"Get to the point," I said, starting the car.

"You're dating Andi, right?" Hannah asked. "You've gone out with her, like, a dozen times in the last month. And then you and Ryan broke up."

"We're… something." I reversed and drove out of the neighborhood. "She doesn't want to date."

"Why?"

"I'm not ready to come out."

"That's bullshit," Hannah said. "If you don't wanna come out, you shouldn't have to."

"And she shouldn't have to deal with feeling like a secret," I retorted. "Where we're at isn't bad."

I thought about how Andi had looked at me when Lisa was bothering me yesterday. She would have defended me, so I defended her. It was easy. Her company had been the highlight of my day.

I knew she was lying about being okay with… whatever it was we were. And she hated lying. She hated secrets, and I'd turned her into one. She cared about me enough to compromise on her core values. She deserved better than what I was giving her. I didn't need to change, I just needed to stop being so afraid.

I wanted to be with her. I could imagine it. Her and Ryan would get along well. Maddie would love her and include her in everything. Mickey would love how happy she made me.

I pushed those fantasies away. That's what they were: just fantasies I could never hold. What was the point of dreaming when I couldn't change anything?

"But you want to date her?" Hannah asked. I nodded. "Have you tried talking this out with her? You know, like a normal person."

"A) Teenagers don't talk about their feelings unless they're venting to someone who's not at all related to the event. B) No, I haven't."

"*You* don't talk about your feelings," Hannah corrected. "Have you even told Mom and Dad you applied to FSU?"

"No," I said. "And I won't, unless I get in, which I probably won't."

"Come on, doesn't it get exhausting? Keeping all these secrets?"

"What would you know about secrets? Every thought you've ever had is posted online the second you have it," I snapped.

"Maybe I don't have to deal with secrets 'cause I'm not ashamed of anything." Hannah crossed her arms over her chest and turned to face the window.

"I'm not ashamed," I said quietly. "It's more complicated than that."

"If you told Mom and Dad, they'd support you. They're not homophobes. And you're friends with Mickey and Maddie. Neither seem to be anti-gay. Anyone else's opinion can fuck off," Hannah said. "If you live your life by what other people think of you, then it's not your life. It's theirs."

I drove in silence for a while after that, considering her words. Andi seemed happy, being herself. I envied her confidence. She stood out naturally, but in an indescribably indifferent way—as if she couldn't help but be the most amazing person in every room. She was proud of herself. To be herself was its own gift, and she treasured it.

And she was so kind. She barely knew Alex, but she was prepared to go toe-to-toe with *The Grapevine* over outing him. She was new at school and almost automatically had a group of friends she did everything with.

Would I gain that if I came out? The confidence, the community? Did I want that?

"Damn," I said. "Where'd you learn to think like that?"

"I've been in school counseling since freshman year," Hannah said. "It's all about positive mindsets and shit."

"Wait, really? How come I didn't know?"

"Because I'm good at keeping secrets," Hannah said with a smile. "My freshman year, I had an anxiety attack while giving a presentation in Spanish and was sent there. I've been going once every other week since."

"Do Dad and Eleanor know?"

"I think so? Like, they had to sign a permission slip in the first week of school, but I don't know if they actually read it," Hannah said. "I'm fine, though. I just get stressed sometimes and I'd prefer to set healthy habits as a fifteen-year-old than as a thirty-five-year-old."

"That's very sensible of you," I commented as I pulled into Waffle House. "I'll try talking to Andi."

"That's all I'm asking," Hannah said. "And maybe look at why you don't wanna come out. See if it's because of what you want, or what you think others want."

"I will," I promised.

ANDI

"You're banned from the kitchen!" Alex yelled, turning on his heel to face Rowan. He was red in the face. Sometimes I forgot how ginger he was.

"What? Why?" Rowan asked.

"Brown sugar and white sugar are not interchangeable, for the hundredth time!" he screamed. "I'm going to strangle you—"

"Kinky."

"—if you ruin another batch of cookies. So please, for the sake of our friendship, get the fuck out of the kitchen."

"Do you see how he's bullying me?" Rowan asked dramatically, turning to me. They could start an argument with a brick. It was a gift.

"You deserve to be bullied if you can't read basic instructions," I said. "Go outside and touch some grass or something."

"I'm gonna get Chipotle. Text me your orders," Rowan said as they grabbed their car keys. "Thank you, again!"

Our theater bake sale started on Monday morning. We were going to sell baked goods before school for the entire week to raise money for costumes for the winter play.

Rowan forgot that they signed up to make four-dozen chocolate-chip cookies. Alex signed up to make two-dozen oatmeal-raisin cookies, Jordan signed up to make brownies, and I'd signed up to bring Ziplock bags. I knew my abilities.

This led to Alex and I spending our Sunday baking cookies in Rowan and Alex's kitchen. "I'm going to murder them one day," Alex said as Rowan blew kisses at us and left.

"Hey, can I talk to you about something?" I asked.

"Is it something from the article?" Alex asked.

I shook my head. "I didn't read it."

Alex looked confused. "What?" he asked, leaning against the counter.

"I haven't read the article," I said. "I read the one Cat wrote, but not *The Grapevine* one."

"Why? Everyone else did, even Jordan and Rowan."

"I figured that if you wanted me to know something about it, you'd tell me. I've heard some stuff from it, but it's your business, not mine," I said. "Do you wanna talk about it?"

Alex looked like he might cry. "The article went through years of text conversations between Jordan and me," Alex explained. "My freshman year was really hard. I had just been homeschooled by my parents for a year and a half, and I really only talked to Jordan and Rowan. I felt alone. Hopeless. I hated my body. I knew something was wrong—no, not wrong—just different about me, I guess. I hated when people would call me Alexandra and when guys would look at me."

Alex jumped up to sit on the counter as he continued. It was strange, seeing him be this vulnerable. He was so mature and steady; it was hard to fathom a version of him that wasn't this confident.

"And I was shy enough that some guys thought I was cute, I guess? I don't know. There were a few guys in different classes that were gross towards me. I ended up having to report one when he told me, in detail, everything he wished he could do to me. It was a really uncomfortable year. And then my older brother—the only person I really talked to in the house, the only person I talked to about the guys or how I thought I might be trans—he left for the Army. He didn't write letters to me, just to our parents, and they would read anything I wanted to send to him. I just felt really alone.

"So, over Christmas break, I tried to… I hurt myself," Alex said. "I didn't succeed, clearly," he laughed. "But Jordan found out, and then Rowan. I'm better now, I've actually been going to therapy since I moved here. But that's a big thing that the article was written about. Not that it had any of that context, just that my freshman year I hated high school so much that I tried to kill myself."

Hearing everything *The Grapevine* had written made me sympathize with Alex more than ever. I knew what it was like to have people believe lies about you and to feel out of control of your own life. At the time, I had prayed someone would help me. Maybe that's why I liked Cat so much. She was the heroine I needed before I even met her. She'd given me the opportunity to become one myself and help Alex. I couldn't change the past, but I could help him now.

"I'm trying to find the author," I said. "I'm going to. Cat and I have been working together."

"You don't have to," Alex said. "What's done is done."

"They have material on other people, too. If we can find who they are, we can publish it and give everyone the chance to get revenge."

"Revenge? What are you even talking about?" he asked. "Andi, I don't think this is a good idea."

"If we release their name, then we can take away their power. They're only doing this because they're anonymous," I said. "I don't want Cat to have to go through what you did."

"They have stuff on her?" Alex asked. I nodded. "Is it like what I saw on Friday?"

"Yeah, but not with me. She's scared."

"You really like her, don't you? So, are you two dating?"

"No, she doesn't want to," I said with a shrug. "I told you about my old school. I can't risk that happening again." I would be a secret affair forever before I let Cat feel how I felt last year. I cared for her far too much to cause her that much pain—or any pain, for that matter. I'd rather endure it myself tenfold.

"I get that," Alex said. "As long as you're happy, I'm happy for you."

"You're a good friend," I said.

Alex shrugged. "I know. Now, can you help me remake this cookie batter?"

We threw away Rowan's batch and remade the cookies according to the recipe.

CAT

"I can only stay till two thirty," I said as I entered Ms. Livingstone's classroom. There was a *Fresh Off the Press* meeting yesterday.

"No problem, Cat." Ms. Livingstone walked to the front of her desk to face the group better. There were only four of us: me, Mathew, Julia, and Olivia.

"I have an idea for an article," Olivia said. "So far, Florida is banning, like, a fuck-ton of books—"

"That's a dollar," Livingstone interrupted.

"Can I write an article about it?" Olivia asked. "I've already drafted the text. Around two hundred fifty words, short and sweet. It doesn't directly state that they're banning queer books or authors of color. I want to do this."

"People will still assume we're taking a political side," I countered. I imagined the girls from cheer reading this and blaming me.

"You got to do your stuff with Alex and Andi; I don't see why I can't write this," Olivia said. "It was pretty clear we took a stance on Alex's stuff."

"What? Are you gonna say we should be pro-outing?"

"No, but if we can publish that, we can publish this." "Are you planning on doing it anonymously?" I asked. Olivia shook her head. "Then that'd be the difference."

"Please, everyone knows you wrote Alex's piece," Olivia snapped. "And even if they didn't, you still approved it."

"We should take a vote," Julia proposed.

I thought about the book bans while Olivia gave her argument to the club. I'd seen TikToks about them, and I'd read the district reconsideration list after trying to check out a library book that I then discovered wasn't there.

The bans were biased against queer authors. Their works were questioned far more than those of straight writers. Popular, award-winning novels written for young audiences were banned for 'pornography' that didn't exist, and there was no law mandating that one had to read a book before challenging it.

"We should do it," I said, before Olivia could take the vote. "But I'd like you to mention that the policy is flawed because it doesn't state that the school board has to read the books it bans. And, you're right, about the Alex article. So, we could make this the feature for the week and bring it up to five hundred words, if you want."

"Really?" Olivia looked suspicious. "What made you change your mind so soon?"

"I need to work on not caring what everyone thinks all the time," I said. "So, let's publish the article. Send it to me on Tuesday, and I'll put it in."

"Unedited?" Olivia asked.

"There can't be any inappropriate language, hate speech, or sexual language," Ms. Livingstone said. "Those have always been the guidelines, according to the principal. Other than that, you're good."

"Great! Thank you!" Olivia beamed. She turned and hugged Julia. I smiled, looking at my phone. Andi had texted that she was working from two to six and sent a selfie of herself in her uniform and a photo of her dog, Poppy, in her Bookmark hat. Andi was so cute.

"And now she's texting her boyfriend," Julia teased, smirking at me. My face went red as I put my phone in my pocket.

"Okay, back to the article," I said, trying to change the topic. We ended up working on it until I had to leave for cheer practice. Olivia promised to send me the finished copy by tomorrow at noon.

ANDI

My shift was pretty easy. We had some new books I had to put up (how Rick Riordan has written so many books is beyond me) but other than that it was pretty slow. We had a book club come in and we got them a box from the back containing their monthly books.

Apparently, Marie had made a deal with them a few years back because she can buy the books in bulk for cheaper than the club can buy them individually. She'll get the books as long as they tell her which title they need at least two months in advanced.

"Are you good to close on Thursday?" Marie asked as I clocked out.

"Yeah," I said. Marie smiled and said good night as I headed out to my car. I blasted *1989 TV* on the way home. I loved the Bookmark. I really needed to make it up to Alex for getting me the interview.

My first paycheck was last week. It wasn't bad, it just wasn't as much as I thought it should be. I forgot to calculate how much I should have earned, but I'm pretty sure taxes took out way too much. Or maybe that was normal. Taxes suck.

I had a frozen chicken pot pie waiting for me at I got home, and a strawberry Fanta in the fridge I was looking forward to.

I smiled, imagining myself curled up in bed eating dinner and watching *Brookly 99*. I'd always had a soft spot for sitcoms. They're predictable. Even when something goes wrong, you can always trust that they'll have a happy ending.

My dad and I used to watch *Friends* together. I'd come home and he'd be watching it in the living room. If I sat down with him, I didn't have to start on homework immediately. That lasted till around 5th grade when he got too busy with his job.

I parked the car and got out. I'd already been home to drop off Peter, but I hadn't seen Mom and Dad yet. I heard them before I saw them.

"I saw you fucking texting her!" Mom was yelling upstairs. I rolled my eyes. I entered the kitchen to see a pizza box on the ground. They probably ordered pizza and then got into a fight. Poor pizza. Thankfully, it was closed, although Poppy was doing her best to open it.

"You're a crazy bitch! She's my friend, which you would know if you had any!" Dad yelled. They always argued like children. It happened at least twice a month. They used to tell me when I was young that it was because they loved each other so much. They gave up that on that once I turned 16.

I grabbed my chicken pot pie and microwaved it. I heard something get thrown and Mom screaming at Dad to get away from her. I used to be worried about that when I was younger. It took me years to not be afraid of Dad after the first time. That was until I came home from school to see Dad with a black eye from a argument with Mom.

I wished the world was black and white. That there was a clear, undeniable distinction between the good parent and a bad parent. But it's not, so I just don't care. If I get too caught up in being the judge, I'll forget that they're still my parents. Sometimes I want to.

I put pot pie in a bowl and grabbed my drink before heading out to my car. I moved the driver's seat back as far as it could go and started the engine. I called Cat. She should be off of cheer rehearsals by now.

"Hey!" She answered before the second ring. "What's up?"

"Nothing, just bored," I said as I opened the Fanta and took a sip. "How was practice?"

"Not bad," she said. "Didn't commit homicide, so I'd call it a win."

"Oh, yes. Homicide or suicide, the bar really is on the ground, ain't it?" I asked, causing us both to laugh.

"How was work? Any crazy customers?"

"At a bookstore? Fuck no," I laughed. "I did have to help a little kid find a Kate DiCamillo book. He called her Katie Cambilo, which was adorable."

"Who's she again?"

"She wrote *The Tale of Despereaux* and *Because of Winn Dixie*."

"Oh my god, she wrote The Tale of Edward something, right? That book about the China rabbit doll?" Cat asked. I beamed.

"Yeah, that's her," I said. Almost nobody knew that book.

"I loved that book as a kid. It made me bawl my eyes out in 2nd grade. That and *Charlotte's Wed.* Like, who choose those books for kids?" She asked. "Sorry if you can't hear me really well, I just got out of the shower and I'm brushing my hair."

"Damn, should have FaceTimed."

"I'm dressed."

"Still," I said. "You look hot with wet hair."

"Simp."

"You're an asshole."

"You don't mean that," Cat said. She was right. "What're you doing?" I was beaming and feeling happier than I had all day.

"Eating dinner in my car. Car dinner. Really classy," I said, smiling.

"Why are you in your car?" Cat asked.

"My parents are going at it and I don't wanna hear them."

"Ew, that's gross," Cat said. I realized how my words sounded and rushed to correct myself.

"No, no, ew. That's gross. They're fighting," I explained.

"About what?"

"Who fucking knows, probably something stupid. They'll be asleep in a couple hours."

"Do they fight a lot?"

"Not really," I said. They didn't fight every day. It could be a lot worse. "You know how parents are."

"I don't think my parents have ever gotten into a fight I can hear. They get into disagreements and shit, but they talk it out in their bedroom."

"Well, so are my parents, they just talk a lot louder," I joked. Cat didn't laugh. "Anything happen at *Fresh Off the Press*?"

"Oh my god, yeah," Cat said, launching into a story about book bans and her helping to publish an article after Olivia writes it.

"That's fantastic," I said. "I'm so proud of you for this." I wished I could hug her and see her and kiss her. She made everything better.

"It's not that big a deal," Cat said, but I could hear the pride in her voice. "I did some research into it, and Olivia's right, the laws bullshit."

"You're gonna be a great journalist one day," I said. I wished I had the passion she did. I wanted to find something I loved as much as she loved writing. The closest I'd gotten to that passion was how I felt when helping Marie at The Bookmark, but that was more due to the company then the job.

"What do you wanna do?" Cat asked. Her question made me realize I had fallen silent.

"I'm thinking about apply at USF for entrepreneurship," I said. "I wanna learn how to run my own business." I'd done some research into entrepreneurship after my conversation with Marie. I liked the idea of running my own business and being my own boss.

"What would you sell?" Cat asked.

"No clue," I said. "Maybe I could open a bakery or a paint studio or a bookstore. I could do anything and be my own boss."

"I can see that for you. I think you'd be great."

"Thanks," I said. That shouldn't make me feel so… happy. I heard some girl yell on the other side of the phone.

"Be down in a minuet!" Cat shouted back. "I'm sorry, Andi, I gotta go downstairs for dinner.'"

"No problem," I said, but felt sad. I could have stayed up talking to her all night, and still miss her. "See you tomorrow."

"See ya!" Cat said as she hung up. I finished my dinner in the silence of the car before going back inside.

CAT

After practice on Tuesday, I headed to Maddie's house. Her ankle was healing well, so hopefully she'd be able to compete after fall season. She always liked fall season more than winter season, though.

Maddie's dad and brothers were at work, so it was just the two of us. "What'd ya wanna do?" Maddie asked as she opened the door. "Are you driving yourself home?"

"Yeah," I said, following Maddie to her kitchen.

"I can't drink by myself," she complained.

"How're you doing?"

"Pretty shitty, Cat," Maddie said. "At least Stacy's been here almost every day," Maddie smiled at that. I wondered if Andi smiled when she mentioned me. If she wove my name into conversations it didn't need to be in just so she could smile at my name crossing her lips. I knew I did with her.

"I'm seeing someone," I said as I grabbed the orange juice from the fridge and poured us both glasses.

"Thought you had a boyfriend," Maddie said, stuffing a fistful of Doritos into in her mouth.

"How don't you know basic manners?"

"I do, I just choose not to use them. Anyway, Ryan?" Maddie asked.

"We broke up," I said. "Realized it wasn't gonna work."

"Cause he's a guy, right?" Maddie asked. I nodded. "Cool. So, you're a lesbian?"

"Yeah," I said. "I'm a lesbian."

"Lost your gold star," Maddie said, leaning back in her chair so far, she almost fell. I rolled my eyes.

"I didn't sleep with him, so technically not."

"Really? He seemed like the type that'd wanna fuck on prom night," Maddie said, holding a strand of her hair in front of her face and admiring the curl pattern. "Oh, I swing both ways, by the way."

"Clearly," I said, referring to the way she was sitting in the chair backwards. She laughed and grinned at me.

"Ya know, I always thought we'd end up… something," Maddie said, then waved her hand dismissively. "So, who's the girl?"

"It's a secret, you can't tell anyone."

"Clearly," Maddie said. "Stacy and I tried coming out, but decided not to after some dick bag grabbed her ass in the hallway and said he found it really hot, the idea of her having sex with a girl."

"Fuck, really? Who?" I asked.

"She didn't know his name so the teachers couldn't do anything," Maddie said, shrugging. She seemed too relaxed.

"Have you been drinking?" I asked. Maddie shook her head.

"I did have an edible, like, an hour ago," she said. "It's for the pain."

"Yeah, right," I said. "Did you at least get it prescribed?"

Last year, Maddie decided to pack a bag of weed to our overnight cheer competition in Texas. She didn't tell me until we were going through TSA. We had to rush to find a way to stuff it in a carry on without being noticed. After we were cleared, I marched her to the bathroom and forced her to throw it away.

"By a family friend, yeah," Maddie said with a shrug and a smile. "You should try some."

"No thanks," I said. "Oh, Andi. Her names Andi."

"Stacy owes me 20 bucks," Maddie laughed. "I told her you liked her."

"What gave it away?"

"The way you talk about her. You don't have a lot of friends, Cat. It ain't a bad thing, but really. It's me, Mickey and Ryan— well, kinda. So, when you're suddenly talking about Andi night and day, it's a bit obvious."

"Hannah's my friend too."

"She's your sister, she doesn't count," Maddie said. "That's like saying Ginger counts."

"I'm friends with Ms. Livingstone," I said, but it even sounded sad to me. "Yeah, I heard it."

ANDI

"Andi, OG *X-Men* films or the new cast?" Jordan asked as they scrolled through Disney+. Jordan, Alex, Rowan and I were over at Rowan and Alex's place to watch the X-Men movies before Alex could watch *Deadpool & Wolverine.*

"I say OG cast," Rowan weighed in. "Cyclops, Wolverine and Jean Grey are hot as fuck. Great polycule rep."

"They're not canonically in a polycule," I argued. "Plus, don't the films end with Jean Gray dead?"

"We don't talk about the third one," Alex said. "It's like the Percy Jackson movies."

"What?" I asked, playing into the bit. "Anyway, I like *First Class* more. Jennifer Lawrance as Mystique, I mean, damn. And Cherik's endgame in my mind."

"Thank you!" Jordan said. "Have you seen *Dark Phoenix*?"

"It's okay," I said. "*First Class* and *Days of Future Past* were the best."

"I like the Wolverine movies," Rowan said.

"That's 'cause you like Hugh Jackman," Alex said. "'Cause you have daddy issues."

"What does that have to do with him?" Rowan asked.

"Hugh Jackman's like, 55, right?" Jordan said. "He and Will Ferrel are around the same age."

"No fucking way, Will Ferrel's old as shit," Rowan said, and then they proceeded to google it. "Son of a bitch!"

The oven timer for the pizzas started going off. "I'll get it," I said. Alex and I got a meat lovers pizza while Rowan and Jordan got a cheese pizza.

I knew where everything was in the kitchen from baking in it with Alex, so I easily got the pizzas out of the oven. The only problem was that I forgot that the oven doesn't have a latch. Instead of staying open, it closes slowly after it's been opened.

I got out the first pizza easily, but the oven door lifted shut into my forearm as I got out the second pizza, causing me to yell and drop it.

My arm hurt as I pulled it away from the heat, cursing under my breath. I didn't even want to look at it. I'd dropped the pizza on the bottom of the oven. It was going to burn, if it hadn't already. Jordan and Rowan were going to be so pissed at me. I ruined their dinner.

I opened the oven door and tried to use a spatula to pull out the pizza, but it fell apart into two halves when the door closed again.

"What happened?" Jayma, Rowan's foster mom, asked from the doorway of the kitchen.

This was the part I hated. The screaming. She'd yell at me for dropping the pizza until I was in tears, and then she'd yell at me for that, too.

I was fine being yelled at, I deserved it. I had experience with it, I knew how to block it out when it got to be too much. But I couldn't bare Alex, Rowan, and Jordan to know how much of a fuck up I was. I didn't want them to hear me cry.

"I'm so sorry, I dropped the pizza, I'll run out and get a new one—"

"No, I mean your arm," she said, walking up and grabbing me by the wrist, being careful not to touch the burn. I pulled away.

"I was stupid," I blurted out. "I forgot that the door closes. I can get the pizza out before it burns-"

"Forget the pizza, let me see your arm. I'm a nurse," she said and holding out her hand. She didn't seem pissed, or even upset. I showed her the burn. "Damn, pretty nasty burn. We need to put it under water," Jayma pulled me closer to the sink.

"It's fine, really," I tried to say. Jayma responded by running the lukewarm water over my arm. I swore, closing my eyes. I clinched my jaw and tried not to curse.

"Doesn't hurt, huh?" she asked sarcastically, raising her eyebrow. At least now I know where Rowan got it from.

"I'm sorry for screwing up dinner," I mumbled, looking away.

"It's not your fault," she said. "We can give Rowan some cash and have them run out to get pizza or something for themselves and Jordan. They won't starve."

' "But it's a waste of money—"

"What? You calling me broke?" She teased with a smirk. "It's fine. Really."

I tried to relax. I was normally good at reading people's moods. With parents like mine, it was a skill I needed. Jayma didn't seem upset. I thought that because Rowan and I had so much in common, our families would be similar. Maybe their biological family was like mine, but they struck gold with having Jayma as a foster mom.

"Okay," I said, looking at the burn for the first time. It was probably two inches wide and a bright red.

"It'll probably blister," she said. "I'm gonna get the aloe from the bathroom. Don't take it out from under the water."

"Yes ma'am," I said as she left. Soon after, Rowan came into the kitchen.

"Oh my god, what happened? Are you okay?" They asked, seeing the burn. I explained what happened and apologized. "It was a mistake," they said.

"I shouldn't have—"

"Not your fault," Rowan said dismissively. "Jor and I can have sandwiches. Really class it up with some PB&Js."

"Fancy," I teased. This felt natural. I liked being able to fall into this banter with them. I knew what I was supposed to say, and they were predictable in the best way.

"Yeah, might even use blackberry jelly."

"Cause you hate good food?"

"What? What's wrong with blackberry jelly?" They laughed.

"Nothing, just strawberry is so much better," I said. Rowan laughed as Jayma came into the room and finished cleaning my arm while they made PB&Js.

CAT

"How do you even play this?" Andi asked as she moved the controller around. She had already expressed her deep disappointment in me for owning an Xbox instead of a PlayStation.

"You shoot shit," I said, showing her the controls. "You don't play video games?"

"Not really," Andi answered. "Remember in elementary school ,when they made us write those essays about how dangerous video games are? That shit traumatized me."

"Wasn't it, like, games would make us into serial killers or something?" I asked as I blew someone's head off.

"The argument was that violent games would make us… fuck, what's the word?" She shot at someone and blew their skull into chunks. "Like, desensitized to violence. But they said it fancier than that."

"The news does that to us already," I commented. "Although I'm sure there is some merit to the argument."

"You could research it for the next paper."

The book ban article had been published that morning. It didn't go over too well, with a bunch of students posting about how *Fresh Off the Press* had a' leftist political agenda'. I thought it was unbiased, but then again, I was biased.

"Olivia wants to do something on her cover band," I said. "And I think Matthew wants to do something on the Superbowl."

"Isn't that not for a couple months?"

"Yeah, but he wants to do a short section on football every week. Like, scores and who looks like they're gonna make it to the playoffs," I said. "He's gonna do it for the NFL and the Dolphins."

"That's our team's name? The Dolphins?"

"Well, one of the teams we play against is the Frogs, so it could be worse," I said, making us both laugh. "You like football?"

"It's okay," Andi said. "I like hanging out with my friends at the games. Getting walking nachos and seeing you and Jordan perform is what I like."

"You still got a thing for my cheer uniform?" Andi blushed but turned to me.

"Yeah, like, a lot," she said. "Don't get me wrong, I've never seen you in something I don't like, but that uniform... Damn."

"Flirt," I teased as I elbowed her. She laughed and smiled at me. Andi was effortlessly hot. She always had messy hair that was never oily. Just curly and wild, like she just rolled out of bed. She always had smudged black eye shadow that made her eyes look impossibly green.

I put my controller on the ground and leaned over to kiss Andi. She dropped hers too, and started to apologize before I pressed my mouth to hers to silence her.

I moved so I was on her lap and she leaned back onto the bed. We pulled away so she could lean against the headboard. "You're really hot, like, all the time," I said as I kissed her neck. She gasped and put her hands on my hips.

"Fuck, Cat," she whispered as I started kissing a part of her neck just below her jaw. "Don't leave a mark."

"I won't," I promised, leaning in to kiss her again. I felt her hands move to the bottom of her shirt. "You don't have to," I told her. She'd said she didn't want to earlier, and I wanted to make sure that she was doing this because she wanted to, not because I did.

"I want to," Andi assured, lifting her shirt over her head. She was in a dark-purple lace bra. I'd seen girls from cheer shirtless before, but this was completely different. I kissed my way from her neck to her chest, wanting to kiss every inch of her bare skin.

Which, of course, was when the door opened. I threw myself away from Andi, almost falling off the bed. She grabbed her shirt and held it over her chest.

Mickey stood there, blinking as if stunned. "Sorry, I'll go," he said, shutting the door. Andi turned to me, confused and pissed.

"You said nobody was home," Andi snapped as she puller her shirt back on.

I should have told him weeks ago. I should have told him first.

I just didn't want his judgement. I didn't want his opinions or his advice, although I probably needed it. Andi looked pissed at me. "Do you not know how to lock a door? Twice, Cat."

"I'm sorry," I said. I didn't want her to be mad at me.

“Nobody was, he has a key,” I said. “I’m sorry, he won’t—”

“I’m not worried about him telling anyone, Cat. Have you come out to him yet?” Andi asked. I shook my head. “He’s probably gonna be hurt.”

“Why?” I asked, but I knew the answer.

“He’ll think you didn’t trust him, or that I’m just… some secret experiment,” Andi said. “You can tell him that, ya know. I won’t be that upset.”

“I’d never say that.”

“That’s what you told me about Maddie,” she countered.

“Well, the kiss wasn’t serious. It wasn’t a relationship,” I said, immediately wishing I could take it back.

“We’re not in a relationship,” Andi snapped, grabbing her bag. “I’m gonna head home, I have a Trig test tomorrow I gotta study for anyways. See ya.”

“Text me when you get home?” I asked as she opened the door.

“Yeah, I’ll text ya.” She left without turning around. I really needed to talk to Mickey.

ANDI

The trig test was a disaster. I should have opted out of a math course this year. I actually considered emailing my counselor to ask if it wasn't too late to drop the class.

I wasn't hungry at lunch, so I just got cheese fries and a Fanta and sat down with Alex, Rowan and Jordan outside. "I gotta go to the band room," Jordan said as I sat down. "I missed a day so I need to rehearse for a bit."

"Can I come with?" Rowan asked. "I'm bored."

"Y'all wanna come? I'll just be in the bus parking lot throwing a rifle and running for half an hour." Jordan said.

"Sorry, skipped breakfast and I'm three seconds away from hangry," Alex said as he bit into his cheeseburger. Well, one of his cheeseburgers. He had two on his plate.

"Andi?" Rowan asked. I shook my head.

"Nah, y'all have fun, though," I said. They shrugged and left. "Weird question, you ever get jealous?"

"Of Rowan and Jordan?" Alex asked. I nodded. He took a deep breath before responding. "Honestly, sometimes. But if Jordan didn't want to be with me, they wouldn't be."

"How did you and Jordan come out? Or deal with that?" I asked, looking over to where Cat was sitting next to Ryan, laughing at something he was saying. I knew they were only friends, but it still stung, that she could be that happy with him and not me. Publicly, at least.

"We didn't really decide to. We still don't kiss at school or hold hands a lot. But we don't try and hide it. Like, if anyone looked, it's clear, but strangers can't tell," Alex said. "Some people still think we're lesbians. Or that Jordan is cheating on me with Rowan 'cause they're more public."

"I've never been in a public relationship," I said. "I was with a girl at my old school, but that didn't end well. And before that, I dated a guy, but we went to different schools."

"I forgot you liked guys," Alex laughed. "I've only ever dated Jordan. Well, unless you count this three-week long thing with a guy in middle school. His name was Onterio and he was pretty nice, but then we broke up over winter break. We were 13, so I don't really count it."

"Is that strange? To have only dated one person?" I asked.

"Kinda? I don't know, Jordan's everything I like in people. They're every good attribute and pop culture reference. They're just really cool and I love them and I love spending time with them. I trust them and they've never made me feel bad about myself. I've never felt like I had to hide any part of myself from them because they love everything about me," Alex shrugged. "You ever been in love?"

"Think so," I said, my eyes finding Cat again. "Not sure, though. I don't know if she likes me back."

"Are you talking about Cat?" Alex asked. "She likes you a lot."

"I just… She's trying, with the coming-out stuff. I get it, I do. Coming out is serious, but it just… It makes me feel like shit sometimes. Like I'm some secret she's keeping. While everyone thinks she's with Ryan, she's actually with me. Don't get me wrong, it's hot most of the time. But sometimes it isn't."

"What's brough this on?" Alex asked. I explained what happened last night with Mickey. "You should talk to her." he said.

"What if she ends this?" I asked.

"This is your last year of high school," Alex said. "You can spend it feeling like someone's secret, or like someone's girlfriend. Your pick."

"Ass," I said as I drank my Fanta. "Fine, I'll talk to her."

Alex was right. No matter how incredible Cat was, this wasn't about her. I didn't need her to announce it to the entire school, but I didn't want to be her 'friend who she makes out with'. I was worth more than that.

"See? I give amazing advise," Alex said with a wink, making us both laugh.

CAT

I knocked on Mickey's door on Thursday morning before school. He was supposed to be at my house by now so I could drive us, but he hadn't showed. Because he's dramatic.

""'Morning," Mickey grumbled as he opened the door. "What do you want?"

He was in pajama pants and a hoodie, but he had his backpack on. His arms were crossed over his chest and he was glaring at me. He dressed shitty on purpose to piss me off when he was mad at me. He knew I hated it, but I wouldn't say anything if I was in the wrong.

"Are you going to school today?" I asked, crossing my arms. "If you're pissed at me, you can say something instead of being dramatic."

"I don't feel well," Mickey said.

"You were fine yesterday," I shot back. "You have, like, 2 minutes to get in the car before I leave you."

"Fine." Mickey snapped and slammed the door. I rolled my eyes and went back to my car. Mickey showed up and threw his bookbag in the back seat. "Where's Hannah?" He asked as he got into the passenger seat.

"She decided to walk with a friend," I said. I took a deep breath. "I should have told you about Andi."

"Why didn't you?" Mickey asked, looking out the window.

"I don't know," I said. "It felt like it would change everything if I told you."

"What would it change?" Mickey asked.

"I just felt like I'd have to prove it to you. That I'm actually gay and this isn't just a phase. I mean, you talked a lot of shit about that girl from middle school that came out as trans and then detransitioned. You have a tendency to gatekeep being queer, Mick."

"No, I don't," Mickey said. "I'm just confused. Why were you with Ryan? Does he know? Are you cheating on him? Does Andi know? Are you two dating or just screwing?"

I took another deep breath. I was prepared for questions. "Ryan knows. I told him a few weeks ago," I said. "Which is a whole another story that I'll tell you in a bit. I'm not cheating on him. Andi knows that Ryan and I aren't dating, and Andi and I are… something. We're not dating."

"You got into a situationship? Damn, who are you?" Mickey said. "Why did you tell Ryan first?"

"I liked Andi," I said honestly. "And I didn't want her to feel like the mistress."

"Yeah, 'cause her being the secret girlfriend- wait, the secret 'not-girlfriend' is so much better," Mickey said sarcastically. "Are you bi?"

"I'm a lesbian," I said. "I've known for a bit, but I don't know, it just- I didn't know anyone I wanted to date, so I thought maybe it was just that I thought some girls were pretty, and that was normal. But then Ryan asked me out and I realized I didn't like guys at all."

"Weird take, but okay," Mickey joked, causing me to smile.

"So, we're good now?"

"One last question. Who else knows?" So, I explained everything to him. About the party and the blackmail and Andi and I. "So, what I'm getting is, you need a hacker?"

ANDI

Closing wasn't as bad as I thought it'd be. I just needed to run through a checklist and make sure everything was clean and locked before I left. It did make me get home around 11, though.

I wasn't expecting anyone to be awake, so I was surprised to find Mom in the kitchen. "Where were you?" She asked. Her voice was strung out, like she'd been yelling. Her eyes looked a little wild. I didn't want to deal with this tonight.

"Work," I said as I hung my keys up on the rack.

"Where?" Mom asked. I fought the urge to roll my eyes.

"The Bookmark, the bookstore down the street." I answered.

"Who told you could get a job? You didn't run it by your father or I? What do you even need the money for? God knows we pay for everything for you," she snapped. I used to get really upset by the stuff she said. At this point, I just put on a blank face. She didn't want answers. She wanted to feel validated.

"I'm sorry," I said. "Did you have dinner?"

"Why did you get a job?" Mom seethed.

"I wanted to save up for college. Dorms and applications and stuff," I said. Moving out. Freedom. Safety.

"You want to go to college?" Mom laughed, putting her hands on her hips. "I've seen your grades, you're not gonna get in."

That hurt. My grades were good. I was an A and B student. I wasn't a genius, but I was good. Better than Peter who barely passed each grade.

"Can I please just go to bed?"

"No," Mom said. "You're never home and now suddenly you want to run away to college. After everything we've done for you? You know we gave up everything in Tampa because you decided you were gonna try being gay?"

"I am gay," I snapped. "And it wasn't my fault."

"Oh? You're gay now?" Mom laughed. "Is this like how you were gonna learn Spanish, or like how you were gonna be a chef? Or like how you were gonna be an artist? God, your generation just loves labels and being different, don't they? Hey, maybe you can put that on your mother fucking college application!"

I just stood as she went off for almost twenty minutes. My mind drifted. She'd feel bad about this tomorrow. She'd probably put $50 into my bank account to spend at the football game and the following party.

After a while, Mom screamed something at me about nobody caring about her and left to her room. I just went to mine, threw my clothes on the back of my desk chair and went to sleep.

CAT

I woke up to Mickey texting me about a post from *The Grapevine.* I felt my heart jump to my throat. This was it. I was destroyed.

New Kid Andrea is Secretly Dating Michael Jang.

Who's Michael? I skimmed through the article until I saw a photo. It was of Andi and Rowan hanging out together. They did look really close.

I didn't know why it never occurred to me that she could be seeing someone else. We weren't in a relationship. She'd made that clear. Rowan was polyamorous. It wasn't a crazy assumption.

So why did it feel like such a betrayal? I got dressed in a fog. I drove Hannah, Mickey and myself to school. "I told you to talk to her," Hannah said.

"Not helpful," I said through gritted teeth as I parked.

"It's probably not true, it's *The Grapevine,*" Mickey said as we got out. I shrugged.

"I mean, it wouldn't be her fault if it was."

"She doesn't seem like the type to cheat."

"We're not dating, so it's not cheating," I corrected.

"You two aren't nothing, though. I've seen how she looks at you and how she talks about you. She'd be stupid to ruin it. You should just talk to her."

Instead, like the mature almost adult I was, I avoided Andi all day.

ANDI

"You're famous, Andi," Peter said, looking at his phone on the way to school.

"What?" I asked.

"New article about you and some kid named Micheal," Peter said. "Oh, it says your dating your best friend's boyfriend. Scandalous."

"*The Grapevine*?" I asked. Peter nodded. "Fuck them, it's all bullshit. Alex is dating Jordan, and I don't know who Michael is."

"I've seen you with him before," Peter said. He waited until I was parked to show me the photo. It was of Rowan and me at The Treehouse a few weeks ago, when Jordan and Alex went to get drinks. I was leaning against their shoulder and laughing at a joke.

"That's Rowan," I said. It never occurred to me that Rowan wasn't their legal name. "It's bullshit."

"But you are seeing someone, right?" Peter asked.

"What?"

"Come on, you're checking your phone all the time and I've heard ya on call till midnight," Peter said.

"Yes, I am, but it's none of your business," I said as I got out of the car.

"Don't do anything stupid. If they break your heart, I'll break their neck," Peter said, and then he flicked me off and walked away. I smiled and rolled my eyes as I walked to where Jordan, Alex and Rowan were loitering outside of the school. Rowan had their vape pen out and was reading the article.

"I wish I could take an edible before class," Rowan said. "You seen this shit?"

"Of course," I said. "I like Rowan a lot better. Good choice in names."

"Thanks," they said and went back to scrolling. "This writer is a transphobic piece of shit. Everyone knows I go by Rowan. It's in the fucking school computers. They'd have to have known me from middle school."

A lead. Fucking finally. I should tell Cat.

But she'd probably seen the article. And she hadn't texted me to ask if it was fake. Maybe she didn't care. Maybe I really just was an experiment to her and so it didn't matter if she had to share.

"Alex and I are headed inside to get sodas before school starts," Jordan said, grabbing Alex's hand and intertwining them.

"I need a sec, I'll catch up," Rowan said and I decided to stay with them.

"This must suck," I said, leaning against the wall opposite to them. They nodded.

"Fucking hate that name," Rowan said as they took a hit of their vape pen, holding their breath for a few seconds before exhaling. "It's my dad's name, and that man never did shit for me. He put my mom in the hospital more times than I can count. Broke her hip, which got her on those fucking drugs. Then she got addicted and OD'd."

"Fuck," I knew something had to have happened to get Rowan placed in foster care. "Was your mom cool?"

"Yeah," Rowan said. "She was the best. She was a art teacher at the elementary school. Her brother, my uncle Harry, is a fashion designer in LA. That's where I'm gonna go after graduation."

"You're foster parents know?"

"Yeah," they said. "Harry's good. He's came here to visit me a few times and I go and see him one month out of the summer. This summer I worked as an intern at his job. It was pretty cool. I got to help with this fashion-show fundraiser where the tickets were expensive and all the profits were donated to help raise money for green energy shit. And all the dresses were made from recycled items."

"That sounds cool."

"The article is bullshit," Rowan said. "But would you want to go out sometime? Like, on a date?" They looked so nervous. My tongue got caught in my throat.

"I can't," I said. Even though Cat and I weren't official, it still felt like cheating. "I'm sorry."

"Yeah, no problem," they said. "Just figured I'd ask."

"You're really sweet, Rowan." The bell rang before I had to stand around them too long. I all but ran to class.

Cat wasn't talking to me or even looking at me. She probably thought that I was cheating on her with Rowan. I didn't want her to think that. I needed her to know that I'd never do that. That I only wanted to be with her. That I'd take stolen kisses and inside jokes with her over anything with anyone else.

CAT

I still hadn't heard from Andi by the time I got home from the football game. It was around midnight. I snuck upstairs and went to change out of my cheer uniform when I heard something bang against my bedroom window.

I jumped and looked around for something to defend myself with. I settled on a screwdriver I had on my counter from when I was putting together a picture frame. I looked out the window to see Andi sitting on my roof. "What are you doing?" I asked as I opened the window, grabbing her wrist and pulling her inside. She fell into me so I grabbed her waist to keep her up right. After she steadied herself, I took a few steps back.

"Badass screwdriver," Andi said.

"I could have killed you," I said.

"Nah, you couldn't have," she took a deep breath. "I needed to see you."

"Clealy," I teased.

"I'm not seeing Rowan," Andi said. I felt myself relax. "But I'm not happy with how we are," she continued. "I want you to know that I don't wanna be with anyone else. Even if you never want to come out, I'd take it. If you only ever want to hang out and play Call of Duty and talk about books, I'd take it."

"I love you," I said. It didn't feel like such a hard thing to say once I'd said it. I'd realized it a while ago, I just didn't know the word until now.

"I love you too," Andi said. She smiled and looked me up and down. "And that's not just because you're the hottest person I've ever see."

"I know you think I look hot in this," I said, twirling around in my cheer uniform. "But I'd look better without it. Wanna help?"

"More than anything ever," Andi said, leaning forward to kiss me. "I've never done this before." Her hands fell on my hips and moved to the small of my back.

"Me neither," I said as she fell onto my bed with me.

Ryan and I never had sex, and he was the only person I ever dated besides Andi. When I first thought I was gay, I read a bunch of sapphic romance novels, so I thought I knew enough.

I also wanted her. I wanted to feel that close with her, that vulnerable. I trusted her enough. My entire body felt hot and filled with desire like I had injected it into my veins. I wanted to hear how she sounded when I touched her, and I wanted her body all over mine. I wanted to kiss every inch of her body to show her how much I loved her.

I never viewed sex as something two people in love did. My existence was a result of a one night stand. Maddie had lost her virginity when she was 15 with her first boyfriend who broke up with her later that week. I always thought of sex as something two people did because they just wanted to get off.

She changed this for me. She had changed so much of me in the best way possible. I'd never felt desire like this before. Now I knew what people meant when they told you to wait to have sex till you were ready.

I was ready, if it was with her.

"If I'm bad—" Andi said as she threw her shirt on the ground. I leaned forward and kissed her.

"You won't be," I laughed. "It'll be great. 'Cause it's with you."

I woke up at 6 A. M on Saturday for cheer practice. Andi was still asleep on my bed. She was in underwear and nothing else. At least I managed to get into shorts and a t-shirt last night.

She didn't stir as I shut off my alarm. I considered calling in sick from practice. I had been really out of it yesterday; they might believe it. But I did need to give the uniform back to Coach Roe for her to return to the dry cleaner.

I had half an hour before I needed to leave for school. I got up and showered and changed into athletic clothes before waking Andi up. "Hey, come on hon, gotta get up."

"It's a Saturday," Andi said. "If you were a sadist, babe, you should have told me before we slept together."

"I have cheer practice," I said. "And unless you want my parents to find you here, you'll let me drop you off at your house."

"Fuck, your parents. We weren't that loud, were we?" Andi asked, jumping up.

"Well, *I* wasn't that loud," I teased, making her face go red. "You're fine. I've belted the entire Eras Tour set list in here and nobody heard."

"You sing? You're so cute," she yawned. "Where are my clothes?" I helped Andi get her clothes together. "I'm stealing this," Andi said, grabbing a *1989 TV* hodie off of my floor.

"Then I get to steal something of yours," I said, hugging her from around the waist and kissing her neck. "You're short."

"You're a bully. This is verbal abuse," Andi teased as she turned around and kissed me properly. "I'll leave my shirt," she said. She'd been wearing a Magneto Was Right t-shirt.

"Cool shirt," I said as I pulled it over my head. It smelt like her.

"Can we get coffee before we go home? I'll pay," Andi said. I nodded and smiled.

We headed downstairs quietly. Thankfully, nobody was awake yet. Andi and I went to The Treehouse before I dropped her off at her house. "Hey, question," Andi asked as she sipped on her iced matcha. "Are we girlfriends?"

"I want to be," I said.

"Can we tell our friends?" Andi asked. I thought about Rowan.

"Yeah," I said. I didn't mention that Mickey and Maddie knew.

"Wanna go out tomorrow with my friends?" Andi asked. "I wanna show off my hot girlfriend."

The little jealous part of my brain loved that. Being able to show her friends how much I loved Andi. Being able to show Rowan that they didn't stand a chance.

"Yeah," I said. "Wait, can I invite my friends?"

"Who?"

"Mickey, Maddie, Stacy and Ryan," I listed. Andi thought for a bit but agreed. "I'll text them later," I said.

"Oh, I forgot to tell you. I have a lead on *The Grapevine*," she said. "Did you go to middle school with Rowan?"

"Yeah, why?"

"I'm gonna need your yearbook," she said with a grin.

ANDI

"You got everything?" Alex asked as he triple checked the bed of the pickup.

"Yes, hon, for the hundredth time," Jordan said and kissed Alex's cheek. "I've checked at least twice."

"Did you use the checklist I texted you, or your memory?" Alex asked, crossing his arms over his chest. Jordan looked away guilty. It turned out, we forgot towels.

Finally, after Alex checked again and again and again, we got to leave. Alex was driving because Rowan was a danger to themselves and others when behind the wheel, which left Rowan and I to sit in the tailgate with the bags and coolers. Usually, we'd sit in the back seat, but the weather was perfect today.

"Hey, no hard feelings about yesterday, right?" Rowan asked as we watched the road fall away behind us. "I don't want things to get awkward."

"Yeah, no problem," I said. "I actually wanted to talk to you. You know how we're meeting with Cat and her friends?"

"Yeah," they said, looking skeptical. "Andi, you better not have set me up with one of them—"

"I'm dating Cat," I said. They looked shocked for a second and then smiled.

"Makes sense," they nodded. "How long?"

"A couple weeks, I think?" I shrugged. "It's complicated."

"Is she cool? Oh shit, is she mad at me?" Rowan asked nervously. I laughed.

"Yeah, she's cool. You've met her before," I said.

"Oh, yeah. I forgot," they laughed. "Yeah, she's cool." Rowan leaned back against the truck. They were in swim trunks and a baby-t that had a t-rex on it and said 'I'm a cunt-asorus'

"Cool shirt," I said. I was in a one-piece bathing suit dress. I wasn't a fan of the cut because it fit like a baby doll dress, but it was either this or my bikini and I hadn't tanned at all over the summer.

Once we got to the beach, Cat was already there. She was arguing with Mickey about something, her hands in the air and Mickey's arms crossed over his chest. Alex honked at her and she jumped

She saw me and waved, turning to say something to Mickey before running from the beach to the parking lot. "It's empty," Cat said as we parked. "How did y'all even find out about this place?"

"My foster parents go here," Rowan said as they jumped out of the truck bed. Cat helped me down and then kissed me. I grinned and leaned into it.

"Hey," I said, putting my arms around her neck. "What's that for?"

"Can't I just be happy to see you?" Cat asked. I rolled my eyes and kissed her again.

"Okay, now I'm feeling really single," Mickey said as he walked up. I was half expecting Cat to pull away. Instead, she put her arm around my waist.

"Should've asked Aiden to come," Cat said.

"Who's Aiden?" I asked. Mickey rolled his eyes.

"This guy on track that has been messaging me on Insta. He's gay, so Cat thinks we should date."

"He's nice!" Cat said. I rolled my eyes. This is what they were arguing about. I looked over Cat's shoulder to see Stacy, Maddie and Ryan with a cooler full of beers. Maddie was drinking from a solo cup and I spotted a wine cooler.

"I'm not drinking," Cat said, following my gaze. "Driver."

"Y'all brought drinks? See, Jor, I told ya we should have brought something," Rowan said. They were helping Alex get the cooler out of the truck bed.

"You don't even drink," Jordan said. We all headed to where the others were set up on the beach.

"Hey!" Ryan said, waving at us. "I'm Ryan, nice to meet you!" He pulled me into a hug, which just made me feel really short when I realized my face was level with his chest.

"Nice to meet you too," I said. "I'm Andi."

"Oh, I know. Cat wouldn't shut up about you on the car ride here," Ryan teased, causing Cat to elbow him. Her face turned bright red. She was so cute. She was wearing a white bikini with gold beading and a large white beach hat.

"What do ya got in there?" Jordan asked Maddie, nodding to the cooler.

"If you're going in the water, you shouldn't drink," Alex said.

"Fine, I won't go in the water."

"Then what's the point of going to the beach?"

"Alex, relax," Rowan said. "I'll drive if you want to drink." Alex, Jordan and I all chorused our disapproval. "Never mind."

"No offense," Alex said, indicating that he was about to say something offensive. "But I would trust a blind dog to drive safely before I trusted you."

"Jordan, your boyfriend's being mean to me," Rowan said as Jordan popped open a beer bottle and took a swig.

"I'm being honest," Alex said with a playful smirk.

"Wanna play volleyball?" Ryan asked. "I brought a ball."

"I'm down," Rowan said. "But I'm putting it out there now that I have the hand-eye coordination of a blind squirrel.'"

"What does that even mean?" Cat whispered.

"Don't know, just go with it," I said. "I'm cool to play volleyball."

We ended up divided into two teams. Maddie's leg was out of the cast, but still wasn't fully healed, so she played ref. Cat, Jordan, Alex and I were on a team together. Ryan, Rowan, Mickey and Stacy were on the other team.

Apparently, I was terrible at volleyball. I kept on losing my footing in the sand and falling over. Thankfully, Ryan and Rowan were just as bad. After a few games, the good players (Cat, Jordan, Mickey and Stacy) decided to play on their own. which was fine by me. I got to sit down and drink from a cheap wine cooler and watch Cat play volleyball in a bikini.

"Hey," Ryan said as he sat next to me. Rowan and Alex were sitting together and watching Jordan affectionately.

"Hey," I said. I didn't know why he kept coming up to me. Maybe he was one of those straight guys that liked the idea of a lesbian. Maybe he was a perv that thought that Cat and I were hot. It wouldn't be the first time I'd met someone like that.

"You really make Cat happy," Ryan stated matter-of-factly. That was unexpected.

"Thanks," I said, unsure how to respond to that. "Did she tell you—"

"Almost a month ago," Ryan said. "I think. I'm shit with time. But yeah, she told me."

"And you're not pissed? Why?" I asked honestly.

"Not my style," he said with a shrug. "Can't make her like men. And she's a good friend. Didn't want to lose that."

"Most straight guys wouldn't be as cool about this as you are."

"Not straight," Ryan said. "I'm bi."

"Cool," I said with a smile. That checked out. "Now that your single, you seeing anyone?"

"No," Ryan laughed. "Too busy. Unless I'm dating a football player or cheerleader, I'd never see them."

"Can I ask you something that makes me sound like an asshole, and you have to be honest?" I asked. Ryan looked confused but nodded. I took a deep breath.

"Are Cat's fears founded when it comes to, like, coming out and shit? Like, is it really that bad?"

"It can be," he said, nodding. "You saw the shit *The Grapevine* did to Alex and Roman. That's their names, right?"

"Rowan." I corrected, nodding for him to continue talking.

"It might be different for her. Maddie and Stacy aren't out, but everyone kinda gets that they're a couple. But from what I've heard from Stacy, since she replaced Maddie on the team, the members haven't been nice to her. She doesn't know if it's because her and Maddie are dating or if it's because they don't like that she got moved from the bench to the main team."

Cat called my name and I looked up. "Wanna go swimming?" She asked, pulling her hair into a braid. I smiled and got up and nodded. We played in the water until our fingers got pruney and we smelt like sand and salt. "What time is it?" Stacy asked. Everyone was in the water so Jordan volunteer to go and check their phone.

"4:58!" They called.

"I'm hungry," Rowan said. "Anyone want dinner?" We all nodded in agreement and headed back to our bags. Together, we set up the beach chairs and sat around a circle as Rowan passed out the PB&J's we made (thankfully nobody was allergic) and the chips we brought.

"Anyone wanna play truth or dare?" Rowan asked. Everyone vetoed it immediately. "Damn, rejected for the second time." Rowan said, making me laugh.

"What about two truths and a lie?" Alex offered. We ended up playing it for a while. I learned that Maddie could speak Spanish, Ryan could sing all of Hamilton, Mickey wasn't a virgin, Alex loved oatmeal rain cookies, Rowan had never been on a boat, Jordan was a Swiftie, and Cat hated Metallica. I lied that I loved watermelon.

"It's gross!" I said, making everyone laugh. "It's just water that taste like sand!"

"You're so weird," Cat said, smiling and kissing me. It was strange and nice, kissing her in front of people. I felt both vulnerable and safe. It was a unfamiliar feeling, but one I looked forward to getting used to.

We finished dinner and decided to walk along the beach as the sun set. It was nice and romantic. Or at least it would have been if Rowan and Jordan didn't get into a sandcastle building contest that led to Rowan throwing a sand ball at Jordan. Which of course started a sand ball war.

"Not doing that," Cat said as Maddie threw a sand ball at Ryan and ran away once he turned around, leading him to chase after her.

"Yeah," I said. We walked back to the coolers. "So, you got the yearbook?" I asked.

"Yeah, it´s in my car." Cat said. She took out her phone and sent me a text. It was a list of four names. Lisa Thompson was on the top of the list. "This is the cross-referenced list of everyone who was at the party, could have taken the photo of Miracle, and went to the middle school."

"Yeah, what happened with Miracle?" I asked.

"It turned out the photo was taken at a church retreat camp, so it was anyone who went to her church," Cat said. "And it was all seniors, so it didn't really help to narrow it down."

"Hey!" Mickey said, waving as he ran up to us. He was covered in sand. "Y´all taking about *The Grapevine*?"

"Yeah," Cat said as Mickey sat down across from us, popped open a beer, and started downing it. "Carefully. If you get sick, I'm gonna let you drown in your own vomit."

"I cannot believe we're friends," Mickey said, ignoring Cat to look at me. "I found a guy who can get the phone number for the Insta account."

"Wait, really?" I asked. Mickey nodded.

"How much?" Cat asked.

"20 bucks, with the discount from me doing his Walt Whitman homework from Handover."

"I got 20 bucks," I said.

"How can we trust him?" Cat said.

"You'll have to risk it," Mickey said. "But if he says anything, I did take photos of his papers before he turned them in so I could report him for plagiarism." Just then, Ryan yelled for Mickey to come and defend him from Rowan and Maddie.

"This is why we're friends," Cat said with a smile as Mickey got up and excused himself to go with Ryan. "Okay, so first thing tomorrow, we'll go and have him hack the account. And then we'll know who the author is."

"I think it's Lisa," I said. "She's been a bitch to me and Alex. She reeks of godly hatred disguised as love."

"I think so too," Cat agreed. "But we need proof."

"Why?" I said. "She spreads lies about us. Why can't we, to her?"

"That's not proper journalism, we need to make sure that what we´re saying is true," Cat said. "And once we tell everyone who she is, she won't post anything else. Then, we can come out."

"What?" I asked.

"I want to come out once we find evidence of who the author is," Cat said. "I want to go homecoming with you and take you to prom and hold your hand in the hallway. We deserve that shit."

I felt like my heart had exploded. I reached forward and pulled Cat into a deep kiss, holding onto the back of her neck. I tried to expel all of this love out of my body and onto hers, so she could feel it too. By the way she kissed back, I figured she did.

"I think we deserve to go back to your car for a bit," I said, smiling as she gasped and grinned.

"Yeah, me too," she said, taking my hand and dragging me to the backseat of her car.

CAT

Here is her number

I got the text during lunch. It was the phone number linked to the Insta account. "Hey, I'm gonna get a soda, be back in a sec," I said and excused myself from the lunch table.

"Can you let me know if they have the blackberry sparking ice?" Veronica asked. I nodded and went to the lunch line and grabbed a coke. They did have the sparking ice.

I called the number. It went straight to voice mail. "Hi! This is Lisa Thompson, please leave a message at the beep! I'll get back to you as soon as possible!"

Andi was right. It was Lisa.

I went back to the lunch table and sat next to Ryan. "Oh, Roni, they do have your drink," I said. Veronica thanked me and headed up to go buy one.

I felt hollow for the rest of lunch. I though it was Lisa, yes, but that's different than knowing it.

Lisa and I met freshman year. We'd been in school together since elementary school. She led bake sales and tutored middle schoolers. She was a good kid.

She also was the type of person to drive her dad's pickup truck with his TRUMP 2024 flags and American flags around town. I hated that damn truck.

In that moment, I felt nothing but pity for her. When I released this article, she'd deserve it. She'd have earned it. Anyone who she shit-talked in *The Grapevine*, while holding her anonymity like a blade, would now have their shot at her.

She'd written some good projects, though. She'd written about the women's weightlifting coach that was grooming kids. She'd gotten him arrested. But she also outed Alex and deadnamed Rowan and was blackmailing me and Miricle.

Empathy was a tricky thing when applied to human beings. Rarely is someone completely good or completely bad. They're just people. You can't truly understand their actions unless you talk to them. Then again, they can lie. I knew that better than anyone.

I knew what I had to do. I had to get her phone and make sure it was Lisa before telling the school. Journalism was all about getting people the truth. And if there was any chance Lisa wasn't behind this, I couldn't do it to her.

ANDI

The plan was simple. After school, I was going to stay and bump into Lisa when she went to get water. I'd start a fight with her while Cat stole her phone and got it to Mickey. He'd take it to the library and print any evidence we'd need off of it. Then, he'd give it back to Cat before practice ended so Lisa wouldn't know.

It should have been easy. But I was not counting on seeing Lisa crying by the water fountain. "Hey, are you okay?" I asked. She looked up at me and whipped her eyes.

"I'm fine, fuck off, dyke," she snapped. I rolled my eyes.

"You could get a little more creative, I mean, dyke? What year is it, 1930?"

"Fuck. Off," she said through gritted teeth.

"Want a Poptart?" I asked, reaching into my purse. "I can't remember if it's strawberry or hot fudge," I said as I handed it to her.

"Why are you being nice?" Lisa said as she took the pastry. She looked at the wrapper skeptically.

"It's not laced," I said. "I'll split it with you, if you want." She nodded and opened it and handed me one. It was hot fudge.

"Why are you being nice?" Lisa repeated as she took a bite.

"It's the Christian way," I said sarcastically.

"You don't have to make fun of my religion, dick," Lisa snapped.

"I'm Christian too. And I used to think like you do. Well, I didn't bully people, but I really though that there was something wrong with guys that liked guys and girls that liked girls. I though there was something wrong with me," I said honestly. "And I know what its like to have nobody treat you like you're a human being and I'd never do that to anyone."

"I'm sorry I hit you," Lisa said. "I was a bitch."

"Yeah, we all can be sometimes," I said. "Now, wanna talk about what you were crying about?"

"It's personal."

"Nobody'd even believe me if I told anyone," I said. She seemed to consider but shock her head.

"I can't," Lisa said. "I'm sorry." She sounded genuine. What the fuck did she do? "I gotta get back to practice."

"Hey, if you ever do wanna talk," I offered. "I can get you my number, Cat has it."

"We're not friends, Andi," Lisa said. "But thanks." With that, she walked away.

CAT

I felt like running miles after practice. Mickey had texted me to meet him in my car, which means he's got something. I basically sprinted to my car. "What ya got?"

"It's not Lisa," Mickey said. I felt my breath catch.

"What the fuck! We were so fucking close!" I yelled, smacking the steering wheel. I felt like I was about to cry from frustration. I was pissed. It'd taken us over a month to get this close. And that bitch still had the photo of Maddie and me.

"It's Veronica," Mickey said and handed me some screenshots that were printed out. Dozens of pages. Conversations between Lisa and Veronica about the newest article. Lisa though it was funny.

But then it came to blackmailing me and Miricle. Lisa told her to stop and that we were her teammates. So, Veronica threatened to tell everyone that she was one of the girls that the weightlifting coach tried to assault sophomore year.

I felt sick. But there it was, all of the evidence. Lisa was running *everybodyandnobody*, but Veronica ran the webpage.

Why hadn't Lisa told anyone? People would have believed her. Everyone knew that guy was a creep. Or maybe she had. Maybe she confided in Veronica and she'd investigated it.

And now she was holding it against her.

"We're gonna burn her at the fucking stake with this," I said as I read through the sheets.

"You got the article set up?" Mickey asked.

"Yep, just gotta get it approved next Tuesday," I said. "And then she'll be destroyed. We'll see how brave she is now that everyone knows."

"If I were you," Mickey said. "I'd tell the girls she has shit on what your about to do. I read that shit she has on Lisa and Miricle. And that's what she has on her friends. I can't even imagine what she has on strangers."

"She wouldn't risk posting anything once everyone knows it's her," I said dismissively.

"How do you know?" Mickey asked.

"She only does this because its anonymous. And people can't take their pound of flesh with her." I pointed out. "Trust me, it'll be fine."

"Okay, if you think so." Mickey said, raising his hands. "Wanna call Andi and let her know?"

"Hell yeah," I said, pulling out my phone to call Andi. She was just as excited as I was.

ANDI

"Where are you going?" Peter asked as I grabbed my purse at around 3 P.M after school. "Work?"

"No, don't work tonight," I said. "I'm going homecoming dress shopping."

"Ug, you're going to homecoming?" Peter groaned.

"Yes, fuck face, I am going to my senior homecoming. Are you?"

"Yeah, I guess I'll have to see you there."

"I can't believe we're related," I said as I left. "Bye, love you!"

"Love you too!" Peter said. Cat was in the driveway, leaning against her car.

"Hey!" She said and smiled as she opened the passenger side door for me.

"I can get into the car on my own," I said, but blushed at the gesture.

"I know," she said, getting into the driver's seat and leaning over to kiss me. I leaned forward into her, letting her pull me in by my neck. I still had a hickey there from when we went to the beach, although it was covered in make-up. Her thumb traced it, making me moan into the kiss.

"Ew, disguising," someone said from the back, making me jump. I turned to see Maddie and Stacy in the back.

"Homophobia," Cat said as she checked her review mirror before reversing out of the driveway. I blushed and looked out the window. I'd totally forgotten that Maddie and Stacy were coming with us.

"Stacy and I call dibs on blue," Maddie said.

"What?" I asked, turning around to face her.

"We're getting blue dresses," Stacy said. "Not matching, but kinda?"

"Yeah, I get that," I said. It just occurred to me to ask Cat if she wanted to get matching dresses too.

"I wanna get a really sexy dress," Maddie said. "Like, one that makes everyone wish they were as lucky as Stacy is. Plus, my tattoos look cool as fuck and I wanna show them off."

"Like, low cut or small skirt?" Cat asked.

"Yes," Maddie said. "Also, I'm 100% going to be wearing my Doc Martins. Those things were too expensive not to wear all the fucking time."

"I gotta get something more dress-codey," Stacy said. "My mom wants to post the photos on Facebook."

"Shit, Ellenor probably does, too," Cat said. "I'm gonna have to make sure to tell her I'm gay before homecoming, don't want that to be a surprise."

"You wanna do homecoming together?" I asked. She looked at me like I had two heads.

"I said this last weekend," Cat said. "And we're going homecoming dress shopping."

"Well, ya never know," I said, grinning and blushing deep red. "I thought maybe-"

"Andi, my amazing, spectacular girlfriend, will you go to homecoming with me? As my date?" Cat asked as she stopped at a redlight.

"Yeah, yes," I said, making both of us laugh. She leaned over and was about to kiss me when the light turned green and she had to move.

"What dress do you wanna get?" Cat asked as she pulled up to the mall. I shrugged.

"What ever fits and is on clearance," I said semi-jokingly.

"Really?" Maddie asked. "You don't have a color you like or a style?"

"I like dresses, but I don't wear them a lot," I said, gesturing to my current outfit of cut off jeans and an oversized Dolphins' Cheer hoodie that belonged to Cat.

"We'll find something that you love," Stacy assured as she got out of the car.

"Oh, I like your hair," I said as I stepped out. I couldn't see it in the car, but Stacy had dyed the ends of her hair a teal green.

"Yeah, our school takes Homecoming week really seriously," Maddie said. "Ay, Cat, ya know the days yet?"

"The days?" I asked.

"The week after next is homecoming week," Cat explained. "We have 5 dress-up days leading to the Friday night game and then have the Homecoming dance and the afterparty at the beach."

"Sounds cool," I said. Cat was pulling out her phone and reading off of it.

"The dress up days are: Monday, Cowboy vs Movie star. Tuesday, Surfer vs. Biker. Wednesday, Barbie vs. Ken. Thursday, Throwback. Friday, Dress up."

"Friday's gonna be awesome," Maddie said. "It's an excuse for everyone to wear their Halloween costumes without the school getting in trouble with The Karens."

"What're y'all doing for Halloween?" Stacy asked. "Mads and I are going as Princess Bubblegum and Marceline."

"I'm Princess Bubblegum, because of my princess attitude," Maddie said sarcastically causing Stacy to laugh and elbow her playfully.

"Don't know yet," Cat said. She seemed so confident. Didn't she feel shitty for not knowing all of the answers? I know I did. Maybe a real couple would have talked about this before, but I was new at this.

We ended up at the first store. I headed to the clearance rack and looked through a couple dresses. Cat and Stacy followed me while Maddie talked to the owner about the exact type of dress she was looking for.

"Oh my god, Andi, I can totally see you in this!" Stacy said and held up a spaghetti strap, tight red dress. It looked like someone had wrapped silk around a mannequin and stapled it together.

"I'll try it on," I said, knowing that it would be too tight. It would show off my stomach and the dips of my hips. I picked out a dark purple dress and a couple black one's before excusing myself to the dressing room.

I knew my body was normal. I'd gone through the hate-my-body phase sophomore year. Not a good place to be. I know everyone wasn't a size three. I knew that Cat, Maddie, and Stacy were all athletes. Maddie and Stacy were flyers. Their job was to be small enough to be thrown into the air. Plus, I had things they didn't. Like D cups. And an ass that looked amazing.

I tried on the first dress. The red one. It fit okay, but it was too tight around my stomach. I tried on the other ones. They were all okay, but just had small things I didn't like. The purple one was so low cut you could see my bra. The black one was strapless and I was nervous it'd fall off. The other black one was covered in glitter that was coming off far too quickly.

I hated dress shopping.

I stepped out of the changing room to see Cat twirling in a light pink dress. Never mind, dress shopping wasn't that bad.

The dress had a square neckline and see through lace long selves that gathered at her wrist. The bodice was tight and went down to her knees, with a large lace skirt extending from it.

"Hey," she said once she saw me, tucking her hair behind her ear. "Ya like it?"

"Yeah, I do. Cat, you look amazing, holy shit," I said, causing her to blush.

"Did you get anything?" Stacy asked. I shook my head.

"Wanna look in another store?" Cat offered. "Or wanna stay here?"

"Maybe another store, if it's—"

"Its fine, we've got nothing to do all day," Cat said. "Wanna help me put this back up on the hanger?"

"Yes," I said quickly, causing everyone to laugh as we went into the changing room. I turned around and faced the corner as she changed.

"What's really up?" She asked. "You can turn around; you've literally seen me naked before."

"Wanted to make sure," I said as I turned around. She handed me the dress and I put it back on the hanger as she got dressed. "The dresses made me look fat."

"Andi—"

"I know, fat's just a word and all that shit. I just didn't look good in them," I said. Cat put her shirt on and leaned forward to kiss me softly. I relaxed into her kiss as she pulled away to put her shoes on.

"We'll find something that you feel confident in," Cat said.

We ended up going to two more stores before we found the dress. I was expecting someone to complain as Maddie and Stacy bought dresses and I was the last one. But nobody did.

I hated shopping with my mom because she hated shopping. If something didn't fit, it's because I needed to lose weight or change something about myself. It was never that the clothes didn't fit my body, it was always that my body didn't fit into them.

At the third store, Cat found the perfect dress. It was a deep red satin dress. It was angular at the hips, pulling the fabric to highlight my waste. It had small off the shoulder sleeves, like it was falling off my shoulders.

"Damn, Andi," Cat said as I stepped out. "This is the one, right?"

"Yeah," I said, beaming. "I look fucking hot."

"Hell, yeah you do," Maddie said, making a cat call. "You look amazing. Red is so totally your color."

"Thanks," I said, blushing as I turned in the mirror. "My ass looks amazing." I said, causing everyone to laugh.

CAT

Maddie and I went back to my place after the football game. She still wasn't allowed to be thrown, but she could dance with us. Which she did, in full uniform and makeup, at the home game this week. Instead of going to The Treehouse, we decided to head home.

"I don't want to pretend I like Lisa and Veronica anymore," Maddie yawned as she started changing into her pajamas. I did the same, making sure our backs were facing each other.

"Yeah," I agreed. "I can't believe it's Veronica."

"You finish the article yet?" Maddie asked. I nodded and then remembered she couldn't see me.

"Yeah," I said. "I just, I feel bad. She—"

"She's blackmailing her friends," Maddie said. "Not cool. She's a shitty person."

"Maybe," I said. "Or she's just a kid."

"We're the same age," Maddie deadpanned. She was right. I knew it. She knew it. "Why are you struggling with this?"

"I just don't wanna be the one responsible for ruining her life," I said. "People will hate her."

"It's her fault. You're just telling the truth," Maddie said. "Cat, I love you, but you do this. You care too much about what other people think. You come up with excuses for people's shitty behavior. You're not responsible for anyone but yourself, not me, not the team. Veronica is not your friend. She's a 17-year-old who decided to create a gossip blog to bully, out, and blackmail students. Alex is 17 and he doesn't have parents anymore, Cat. And that's practically her fault."

"Yeah," I said. "Wait, what do you mean coming up with excuses for your shitty behavior?"

"I can be an asshole," Maddie said. "I know it, I'm fine with it. But Coach gets pissed at me and you always come up with excuses. Like, when I showed up to that game last year stoned. You saved my ass."

"That's being a friend."

"That's making yourself responsible for my actions," Maddie said. "Which you're not. Like you're not responsible for Veronica's actions. I know you're our Captain and shit, but you're not our coach. Or our mom."

"Damn," I said, laughing. "You are an asshole."

"I know," Maddie said with a smile. "Now, can we please go to sleep? I'm fucking exhausted."

ANDI

"Hey, Jor," I call from the dining room. "Can you help with this shit?"

"Yeah, sure," Jordan says as they came from the back porch. We were having a final summer BBQ at Rowan's before hurricane season really starts. We had our first flooding yesterday, so we decided to do this before actual hurricane show up.

I hate driving when it's storming. The car's so low to the ground that I can barely see if there is a truck in front of me. It was just their brights on in my face. I swear, I almost got into a wreck coming home last night.

For the record, their version of a BBQ was to grill hamburgers, hot dogs, kebabs of vegetables, and corn. We also made mac and cheese and a bunch of other sides. Ryan, whose family was from Louisiana, grew up with BBQs of brisket and pulled pork. This is not that.

Before everyone got to Rowan's, I was trying to finish my SSAR. My school counselor said that because it's a Student Self Report thing, she can't help.

"Should I put in the high school credits I took in middle school?" I asked, pointing at my laptop screen as Jordan entered the dining room. They had been upstairs in Rowan's room doing god knows what while Rowan's foster parents were cooking. Alex was outside helping Rowan's foster dad man the grill.

"Oh, I don't know. Sorry, my counselor printed out my transcript and my mom inputted it. You should ask your parents for help," Jordan said, as helpful as a foggy mirror.

"I can't," I said, trying not to sound rude. I knew Jordan was trying to help, but they weren't. "My parents aren't like that."

"I'm sure they'd help if you asked," they assured, like they knew my parents. Just then, Jayma came out of the kitchen and looked at my screen.

"Oh, sweetheart, let me help ya. I did this with Alex last week," Jayma said, pulling up a chair.

"Oh, if your cooking—"

"The food's done," Jayma said. "So, you do put in the high school credits from middle school. Here, let me pull up your transcript for ya."

An hour later, I'd put everything in. "Thank you so much," I said as I turned off my laptop and put it in my book bag.

"No problem. So, what colleges are you looking at?"

"I have a list of about 5 that look cool," I said. "Did you go to college?"

"I'm in college," Jayma said. "I'm completing my bachelors online."

"Oh, cool," I said. I didn't know that was an option. "Why?"

"I'm a nurse," Jayma said. "But I wanna get paid more. And I need a degree for the next position I'm applying for."

"Good plan," I said. I still wasn't completely sure how to speak to adults. "I wanna go into entrepreneurship."

"Well, let me know when you get into college," Jayma said. "We're gonna have a party for Alex, we can have one for you too. Rowan's gonna get their party before they leave for LA."

"I don't know if I'll get in," I said, thinking back to my argument with my mom last week. "My grades are okay. You should see Cats; she got a 4 point something. She's brilliant."

"Your gonna get in," Jayma said. "Trust me," she smiled. "Wanna help me with the banana pudding?"

I agreed and she taught me how to layer the pudding over the vanilla cookies. It occurred to me how lucky Alex and Rowan were to have her as a mom, and how they probably knew that.

CAT

I'd stayed up late talking to Andi so first thing in the morning, I went downstairs for coffee. I poured myself a mug and checked the time. I was supposed to get up earlier.

"Hey," Dad said from the living room. "What're you doing up this early? It's your day off."

I turned around to see Dad, Eleanor and Hannah sitting in the living room. I hadn't expected them to be up 8 A. M on a Sunday. I wish I'd worn something better. I was in white shorts and a *TTPD* t-shirt.

"I wanted to talk to y'all about something," I said as I placed my coffee down. It'd have to wait. I went over and waited till Hannah paused the show they were watching.

"Is everything okay?" Eleanor asked. "Is this about Ryan?"

"What happened with Ryan?" Dad asked.

"They broke up, honey, I told you weeks ago."

"Yeah, but its more about me," I said, wishing I'd had the coffee just for something to hold. "I'm seeing someone else."

"Oh," Eleanor said. "Who is he? Have we met him? Is he nice? Is—"

"Mom!" Hannah hissed. "She's talking."

"Sorry, sorry," Eleanor said. "So, who is he?"

"You remember my friend Andi?" I asked. Eleanor looked shocked, and Dad seemed confused.

"I've heard the name, but I can't remember his face. Is he that new Mexican guy you're hanging out with? Or the guy with the green hair?" Dad asked.

"She's the girl with red hair, although it's kinda pink now, I guess," I said. Dad still looked confused. "I'm a lesbian, Dad."

"Thank you for telling us, that means so much, right?" Hannah said. I tried not to laugh. It was so obvious what she was doing.

"How… how long have you been seeing this girl?" Eleanor asked.

"A few weeks."

"We're going to have to meet her," Dad said. "Like, as your girlfriend and stuff. We should take her out to Texas Roadhouse. Wait, is she vegan? I saw online that a lot of lesbians are vegans."

"Where did you see that?" Elenore asked. "But, yes, I agree with your dad. We'll need to meet her. And you're going to homecoming, right? We'll need her over here for photos at least an hour before the event."

"I have a photo of us in our dresses," I said and offered Dad and Ellenore my phone. The photo was of Andi in her dress and me in the blue jeans and tank top I wore to the mall. She was standing up on the pedestal, so she looked taller than me.

"She's not really that tall," I said as I put my phone away.

"You look happy," Dad said. "Are you still friends with Ryan? I'm his Facebook friend but I'll unfriend him—"

"You didn't when you heard they broke up?" Ellenore asked.

"I didn't' know!" Dad argued.

"I told you! Twice!"

"Doesn't mean I knew, means ya told me, they are very different things."

"Ryan and I are friends," I said. "He's cool."

"I'm hungry. Wanna go out to Cracker Barrel?" Dad asked. Everyone agreed and we went to get ready. Hannah walked to my room with me.

"That went great!" Hannah said. "Honestly, I was worried."

"I could tell," I said. I felt freer than I had in a long time, like a weight had been lifted off of my shoulders. All I wanted to do was tell Andi. "I can't believe I just did that."

"I'm proud of you, sis," Hannah said and hugged me. I hugged her back before kicking her out of my room to get dressed and call Andi to tell her all about it.

ANDI

"You don't have to be here," Cat said as we headed to Livingstone's classroom on Monday. "I have cheer in twenty minutes anyway."

"Can I see you in the uniform?" I asked, picturing her in it.

"The Friday after next, I'll own it," she said. "We get the uniforms once field season is over."

"Wow. I'm gonna need a day to process that," I joked, making her laugh. I wished we weren't at school so I could reach out and hold her hand.

"Hey!" Cat said as she opened the door. Ms. Livingstone was at her desk, doing... something teachery and important, probably.

"Hey, Cat!" She said, standing up. "Oh, hi! I'm Ms. Livingstone." She extended her hand to me. I introduced myself and shook her hand. "Do you want to join the newspaper?"

"No, I'm here with Cat," I said, nodding to Cat who was holding the file of all the evidence we had against Veronica, as well as Cat's article. I'd helped tame some of her stuff down, but it was all her work. I was a shit writer anyway.

"What's this?" Ms. Livingstone said as Cat handed her the folder.

"I found the author of *The Grapevine*," Cat said. "It's the gossip blog that outed Alex and has been manipulating students on campus."

"This is… shit, sorry, don't tell anyone I said that," Ms. Livingstone said as she looked through the file. "Cat, what do you want me to do with this?"

"I want to publish it," Cat said, as if it was obvious.

"Veronica's family could sue the school for bulling, Cat. This is a pretty heavy accusation," Ms. Livingstone said. "And how did you even get all of this? You know what, mandatory reporter, I don't wanna know. But we can't release this."

"We need to," Cat argued. "This is important work, this will help—"

"I said no," she said. "Listen, I agree with you with this. But it'll be my job on the line if people get pissed over this. If even one part is false—"

"It's not."

"And unless Veronica divulged this information, you can't release this through the school newspaper. If you want to post this on Facebook or whatever, be my guest. But we can't use *Fresh Off the Press* for this. I'm sorry." Ms. Livingstone said. Cat looked like she was about to cry and stormed out of the classroom.

I followed after her and jogged to catch up with her. "Hey," I said and went to put my hand on her shoulder.

"It's not fucking fair," Cat snapped. Thankfully most students have already left the school so we had the hallway to ourselves. "She gets to say whatever she wants without consequences, and we put in all that fucking work for nothing."

"I can post it to Instagram on my account," I said. "Not everyone might see it, but if Ryan reposts it, it'll get a lot of attention."

"I can't put him under pressure, or you. You'd have a target on your back," Cat said. "God, this conversation is so fucking stupid!"

"I know, I know," I said and Cat let herself be hugged and pulled into my arms.

"I have cheer in ten," she groaned. "And I'll have to pretend like she's not the author."

"I can pick you up after, maybe take you out to dinner." She rested her head on my shoulder and I pressed a kiss to her cheek. She smiled and leaned back. I didn't know what I could do to help her fix this, but at least I could make her smile.

"Oh, speaking of dinner, my dad wants to take you out for dinner sometime," Cat said. I laughed and smiled.

"I still can't believe you told them. You said Elenore wants homecoming photos, right?" I asked. Cat nodded and I laughed. "It's gonna be awesome."

"I wanted to be able to get *The Grapevine* off of my mind before homecoming so we could go together." Cat said. She looked like she was about to cry again.

"Hey, it's not a big deal—"

"It is!" Cat cried, wiping her face. "I want to be able to be a normal couple with you! I want to be able to eat lunch with my fucking girlfriend!"

"We'll figure it out," I said, running my hands through her hair. "Wanna run to The Treehouse after practice?"

"I love you," Cat said as a way of affirmation. I looked around the hallway to make sure it was empty before kissing her.

CAT

I was pissed going into practice, which was never a good thing. Andi offered to stay and do homework in the bleachers, but she'd have to be outside in jeans for 5 hours. Plus, it looked like it was about to rain.

After two hours of practicing, it started to storm. "Okay," Coach Roe said, getting everyone's attention. "We're gonna end rehearsals early. Everyone go home."

I was smart enough to know an opportunity when I saw one. I grabbed my jacket and put my phone in the breast pocket and opened voice memos. I pressed record.

"Hey, Veronica," I called as everyone started getting their stuff and heading to their cars. "Can I talk to you for a second?"

"Yeah," Veronica said. We went under the bleachers to talk. "What's up?"

"I know it's you," I said. She looked scared for a moment and then schooled her face to fake confused.

"What's me?"

"Don't play stupid when I know you're not. *The Grapevine*? Really? That's the most original name you could come up with?"

"It's catchy and easy to remember," Veronica said, dropping the act quicker than I thought she would. "So what? You know it's me? If you tell anyone I'll release your photos. We're at a checkmate here, Cat."

"No, we're not," I lied. At least this lie wasn't going to hurt anyone. "Because I can release to the entire school that it's you through *Fresh Off the Press.* I have evidence."

The key to lying is confidence. I kept my shoulders straight and my chin up. My voice was steady. She needed to know I believed it, so she would. I hated that I knew how to do this so well.

"Like what? How the hell did you even find out?" Veronica asked. "And nobody would even believe you."

"Yes, they would," I said. "Now, I won't release anything if you don't post anything this week. Or ever again."

"What do you even have? How do I know you're not bluffing?"

"I found out it was you by doing a reverse search on the Instagram account or whatever the fuck it's called and then getting Lisa's phone number. Smart. But I found the texts between you and her with your instructions to say everything. And I have them all printed out, and copies that I'll release."

"So what? I'll just deny it," Veronica said.

"Say you'll stop writing, and I'll destroy all of it," I said. "We can forget the blackmailed ever happen. We'll move on. Be a team. Right?"

"Fine," Veronica conceded. "I won't post anything else on the blog."

"Why did you start?" I asked. I'd seen in movies that villains loved to monologue and was really hoping she did, too.

"I started freshman year. It was after 2020, and everyone just felt like they could do whatever they wanted. My rights were attacked—"

"Your rights?" I snapped. "Did they pass a Don't Say Straight bill?"

"That bill was misinterpreted," Veronica argued. "It was to protect kids from indoctrinating liberals—"

"It was to strip children of any safe place they had," I argued. "Have you even read it? It's to enforce parental control."

I took a deep breath. This wasn't a debate about HB 1557. It was about *The Grapevine.* And getting a proper confession.

"You could have joined *Fresh Off the Press* if you wanted to write," I said.

"But I didn't want it to be censored, I wanted to be able to tell people the truth," Veronica said. "You know what I don't owe you a fucking explanation. It's my blog; I can write whatever I want."

There it was. I hid my grin perfectly until after I stormed off. I check the audio as soon as I got in the car. "It's my blog; I can write whatever I want," rang out loud and clear.

I got her. I finally fucking got her.

ANDI

"You look stupid." Peter said as he got out of the car and left to go see his friends.

"Love you too!" I yelled after him, and he flicked me off. I rolled my eyes as I headed to Rowan's truck bed where everyone was gathered around. Rowan was taking a photo of Alex and Jordan posing together.

"Hey!" Cat said, waving me over. She had her hair pinned up and was in a tight pink dress with long white gloves and a fake diamond necklace. "Andi, you look amazing!"

I blushed and looked down. I was in jeans, a flannel, and a cowboy hat.

Rowan was dressed in a… suit? It had a see threw lace top with fabric bundled in the front and the waist of their pants ended just under their chest. I felt like I'd seen something like it before, but I wasn't sure.

Alex and Jordan were dressed similar to me in jeans and cowboy hats. Jordan even had boots with spurs, which was pretty cool. Ryan and Mickey were leaning against Cat's car and talking about something I couldn't hear. Ryan was in a basic black and white tux. Mickey was dressed like a cowboy.

"Hey!" Maddie said as she got out of her car with Stacy. They were both dressed like movie stars.

"Oh my god, where did you get your dress?" Rowan asked Maddie who was wearing what was probably a reference to a red carpet I didn't understand. Rowan and her were talking back and forth about the dress and where she got it and about Rowan's outfit, which was apparently a call back to a Harry Styles met gala appearance from over 5 years ago.

"Anyway," Stacy said, stepping away from Maddie. "You two look great."

"You do too!" Cat said. "I love Homecoming days, they're just the best. The teachers won't give a shit about lessons or absences. Y'all wanna skip before lunch and go somewhere else?"

"Can't," Stacy said. "Junior, remember?" Seniors were allowed to leave campus when they wanted, but juniors still had to be checked out.

"Andi?" Cat asked.

"Sorry, babe. Mom and Dad are already up my ass about me getting a B, can't have the school call them for me skipping."

"Ug, I guess I'll stay," she said, smiling. "Last homecoming week! Can you believe it?'

"Did you snort pure caffeine this morning? Why are you so awake at 7 A. M?" Mickey asked, walking over to us. "Morning, Andi."

"Hey, Mickey," I said as he leaned into Cat's shoulder. She laughed and wrapped her arms around him. I wish I could do that. Just openly be held by her. I took a sip of my coffee as the bell rang.

"Wait, group photo!" Cat yelled. Everyone gathered in front of Cat and Rowan's cars as Stacy took our photo. She'd volunteered, insisting that at least one photo should be seniors only.

"Gotta get to class," Cat said. "I'll see ya later." With that, her and Mickey headed off to first period.

I navigated the hallways by myself and headed to my first period. A bunch of people were wearing floor length gowns, probably just reusing their prom dresses. That's what I would have done if I'd had a prom dress.

I got to first period and took my seat and pulled out my notebook and a novel. After we finished the Pledge of Allegiance, someone tapped me on my shoulder.

I turned to see a girl I'd never met or spoken to. She looked a little worried and excited. "Yeah?" I asked, wondering what she needed.

"Have you read the new article?" She whispered. I felt the blood drain from my face. "Oh shit, you haven't, have you?" She laughed and sat down, as if my world wasn't spinning. I tried to take out my phone, but the teacher told me to put it away or he'd write me up. So, I sat in class, trying not to have an anxiety attack about whatever *The Grapevine* had posted.

CAT

"Hey, are you okay?" Alex said, coming up to me after first period. We had classes next to each other but he rarely talked to me at school.

"Yeah," I said, confused. "Why?"

"Let's go to the bathroom," he took my hand and dragged me to the bathroom.

"Hey, get the hell out—" A girl washing her hands said to Alex but stopped when I walked in. She froze like she'd been caught and hurried out of the bathroom quickly.

"Veronica posted an article about you and Andi," Alex said. I felt like I'd been dropped into a cold lake. Is this how Alex felt when his article came out?

But at least my friends already knew. At least my parents did. But I wanted this to be mine. I wanted to come out with Andi before homecoming, maybe Friday night, and be able to make it perfect. I had time to craft my words into exactly what I wanted to say. I could control everything about it.

"What did it say?" I asked, trying not to cry. I walked to the mirror and used a paper towel to dry my eyes before the tears ruined my makeup.

"It… It's really bad, Cat," Alex said. He took a deep breath and reached out and held my hand. Fuck. "It says a bunch of stuff, but at the end it speaks directly to you. It asks for you to admit whether you were a—a cheating whore, or if you'd been manipulated by Andi, coerced, into being with her."

"Fuck Veronica, I'm going to beat the shit out of her," I said, clenching my fists. I could put my fist through a fucking wall and not care right now. Coerced me? Andi didn't do shit and the fact that Veronica had drug her into this—

"You should check on Andi," Alex said.

"Vernonia has 2nd period weight lifting. I should break her jaw," I said. I could see it. She wouldn't expect it. I could wait until she and I were in the locker room by ourselves and punch her. I could slam her head against the lockers until she was spitting out her own fucking teeth. I could break her hands so the bitch couldn't write another word-

"No," Alex said, grabbing my arm. I fixed my glare on him, then relaxed. I wasn't angry at him. I was angry at Veronica. That's how you manage anger, you keep the destination. You don't let anything distract you. You realize who's good and who's bad and you know that good people don't deserve your wrath. The bad people do. Even if your wrath is words that you wish would turn into a noose for them to hang themselves on.

"What?" I asked.

"You'll get your ass kicked out of school," Alex said. "Trust me, I went over this before with Jordan. You can't be around her. You need to go find Andi."

Andi. Andi, my amazing, incredible girlfriend. I needed to be with her. Yes, that made sense. I took a few deep breaths. I was still angry, but that could wait till later. Had anyone said anything to her?

"Where is she?" I asked. Alex pulled out his phone.

"She went home early," Alex said. "Just texted and asked if I could pick up her work from class."

"Where, though?" I asked. Alex shrugged. I tried to imagine myself as Andi. She wouldn't be at her house. She hated it there.

"I'm going to check on her," I said, getting my keys out of my backpack. "I'll let you know if I can't. Thank you, for telling me."

"I wish someone had told me, instead I got to read that shit myself," Alex said. "And Rowan's on their way to ask Mickey if his hacker friend can get onto *The Grapevine* and delete the article, or post something else."

"Oh, don't worry. I'm gonna post my stuff, and it'll destroy her," I said as I left.

ANDI

I sat at a table in the back of The Treehouse, checking my phone. I'd read the article at least 6 times. I kept on refreshing Instagram to see what everyone was posting.

Riddle179: I knew it, once Cat posted that first article, she was done
Swiftie#13fan: can anyone talk about how invasive this is for Cat and Andi?
NickAbrams: Ha, bet they're hot together.
_Jessica_LittleMissDemure:_ This is so sad, Cat had such a good boyfriend. I really liked their romance.
Ryan#77: Sorry to break it to you, but Cat and I are not together. We broke up months ago. Cat and Andi are a much better fit then Cat and I.

I smiled at Ryan's post. He didn't need to post it, but he did. He also posted a photo of him and Cat from a few weeks ago, saying that they broke up a while ago and were keeping it private.

There were people saying how I'd taken advantage of her after the breakup. How I was an experiment. There were some people that said that it was terrible, what happened to us. But they were few and far between.

Then, Cat's profile photo changed. It was now a photo of her and I from when we went to the beach. She had her arm around me and was kissing my cheek.

Then, her posts came in. The first was screenshots and an audio recording. The next was explaining how Veronica was the author.

The third post was my favorite.

I wanted to be able to post this on my own accord. I'd written it weeks ago and was planning on posting it Friday night, right before Andi and I went to Homecoming together. But I guess Veronica wanted the date moved up. So, here it is.

I'm a lesbian. I feel like that's very important to clarify. I always have been, even when I was dating Ryan. I am a lesbian. I only like women. I dated Ryan because I was scared of what would happen if people knew. But now, fuck it. People should know. If you want to know me and follow me online and vote for me for Homecoming Queen, you should know who I am.

I'm also Andi's girlfriend. We've been together for over a month. And I don't owe anyone details of my relationship.

Veronica outing us isn't the first time she's done something like this. She's homophobic and transphobic and her blog should not be tolerated. Anywhere else, this would be considered cyberbullying. Do not read her blog anymore, please. Do not give her any more attention. It's all she wants. She's just a child acting up for attention who refuses

to take accountability for her actions and the impact they have on others.

What if this was you? What if your private relationship that got called into question? What if you were framed as being a whore or a victim? I am neither, fuck you, Veronica.

"Hey," I heard as I looked up from my phone. I didn't realize I had tears in my eyes until I looked up and they ran down my cheeks.

Cat was standing next to me. She looked like she just cried, her face all red and splotchy. She fell onto the sofa beside me and pulled me to her as I let the phone fall to the ground.

"I'm sorry," Cat said, holding back sobs. "I'm so sorry, if I hadn't said anything about this—"

"It's not your fault," I said, pulling away to wipe her face. "Why did you post that?"

"It's the truth," she said. "I'm sorry I didn't do it weeks ago." I reached forward and pressed my lips to hers. She tasted like salt and coffee. She kissed me back, putting her hand on the back of my neck. And we could do that now. That was something we could do.

We could kiss in public because we weren't a secret. I wasn't a secret. It felt safe, to be held by her like this. As if no matter what happened, she'd be there for me. The craziest thing was that I believed it. I trusted her to stand by me through this, to love me through this.

Wasn't that incredible?

CAT

"Just don't punch anyone," Mickey said as I drove us to school.

"Or yell at anyone. If anyone says anything, you snitch, okay?" Hannah said. "You're a journalist, the snitching should come naturally."

"I'm gonna walk you to first period, and then Alex is gonna walk you to second, and Ryan is gonna walk you to third, okay? Keep your phone on you, we'll text when we're outside."

"Ignore everyone and then come sit with us at lunch." Hannah said.

"I know, we've been texting about this since yesterday." I said as I pulled into school. I was dressed in an oversized Hawaiian button up and denim shorts. Hannah was dressed similar, but her shirt was tied around her waist. Micky was dressed as a surfer, too.

Andi was dressed as a biker. She was in black skinny jeans, a zipped-up leather jacket, leather boots, and her hair was done up with jell. She dyed it again last night. Now, her hair was a magenta-purple.

"Good luck with that," Mickey said as we pulled up and he saw her. "You two agreed no PDA, right?"

"Parking lot doesn't count," I said as I got out of the car. Hannah hugged me and headed off to class. "Hey!" I called and waved to everyone.

"Hey!" Andi said. She had on black lipstick, too. I wondered what it tasted like. I knew her dark purple one tasted like grape. Her dark red one tasted like cherries.

"Hey," I said and leaned against the truck next to her. Everyone else was dressed as bikers. "Ready for this shit?"

"I'm walking you to class, remember?" Ryan said. Andi laughed and nodded. I loved that they were friends. I thought they'd be awkward, but they're not. Ryan's chill and Andi doesn't really seem to care. They're both really big Percy Jackson and Marvel fans.

I just tried to focus on classes throughout the day. I tried to ignore the glances and the whispers. I finally got to relax at lunch though. I took my tray and went to sit down with everyone. We'd all agreed to sit together at lunch. Andi moved her backpack for me as I approached. She was saving me a seat. Maybe this wasn't the worst thing that could happen.

ANDI

After school, Ryan walked me to my car. "This is completely unnecessary," I complained.

"Better safe then sorry," Ryan said. "Don't wanna have to answer to Cat if anyone says something to you."

"Yeah, she's got a temper, doesn't she?" I smiled, thinking of how Alex told me in class that he thought that Cat was really about to beat the shit out of Veronica. He told me that's why he wanted to have people take her from class to class, to make sure she didn't fight Veronica.

"Yeah," Ryan agreed. Peter was leaning against the hood with his air pods in. "Hey!" Ryan said as Peter took out his airpods. "I'm Ryan."

"I'm Peter." Peter said. I rolled my eyes at the awkward introduction.

"Need a ride home?" I asked Ryan. He shook his head.

"Practice for the big game on Friday. You'll be there, right?"

"Obviously, gotta support Cat. And you, too."

"Oh, I'm so offended," Ryan teased as he walked away. "See ya later."

"Ain't he your girlfriends ex?" Peter asked as we got into the car. I rolled my eyes.

"Yeah, but we're friends," I said.

"Why didn't you tell me about Cat?" Peter asked, crossing his arms.

"You don't tell me shit about your life," I countered. "Or whoever you hang out with all the time."

"Fair," Peter said begrudgingly. "I'm seeing this girl name Kiera. She's a sophomore and we're in the same math class. I asked her out to homecoming on Monday."

"Really?" I asked. "When can I meet her?"

"Never," Peter said. "Just so you know, Veronica and I have a class together. She told me it wasn't her who wrote the article and I told her to go fuck herself."

"Thanks." I said. What else was I supposed to say to that?

"Okay, air pods are going back in," Peter said and exited our reality and went into his own, filled with whatever electo-scream-pop music he listens to.

CAT

I headed to cheer practice by myself. Mickey asked if I wanted him to come along. I told him no. He'd just be sitting in the bleachers for hours. Knowing him, he'd get a sunburn right before homecoming.

When I entered the locker room, everyone who was already in there went silent. I was the last one there on purpose. I'd given them time to talk among themselves.

"Hey, Roni," I said casually to Veronica, going to my locker and grabbing my clothes from my backpack. I started changing right there, as if everyone wasn't staring at me.

"What the fuck are you doing here?" Veronica asked, walking towards me. I pulled my shirt over my head. Lisa grabbed her and whispered something in her ear. I could hear it in the silence of the room.

"It's not worth it."

"What do you mean?" I asked, pretending to be confused. "Why wouldn't I be here?"

"We don't wanna change with a fucking dyke in the room," Veronica snarled. "It's disgusting."

"Okay," I said. "Everyone, if you really think I shouldn't be changing in here, feel free to complain to Coach Roe. Tell her what a fucking dyke I am, I'm sure it'll go over well."

"You already got what you wanted. You ruined my life. Why can't you just leave me alone?"

"She ruined your fucking life? Oh my God, cry me a river and then drown yourself in it, you fucking bitch," Maddie snapped, coming to my defense.

"I should have leaked the shit between you two," Veronica said.

"What between them?" Del asked.

"They got drunk and kissed at a party." Stacy said dismissively, rolling her eyes.

"I didn't ruin your life," I stated. "You did. I just told people the truth."

"Then so did I," Veronica said. "You wanna talk about truth? Is that why you dated Ryan for months?"

"If you don't understand the difference between what you did and what I did, then you're an idiot," I said simply. Veronica snapped and pulled her fist backwards to punch me. This is what I wanted. If I could get her to swing the first punch, if I could seem calm and reasonable, it'd be self-defense.

Miracle grabbed Veronica's shirt and pulled her backwards, making her shoulder slam into the lockers. "Don't." I'd never heard her sound so angry.

"You assaulted me!" Veronica cried, holding her shoulder.

"You have no loyalty," Miracle snapped. "If there is anyone I don't want in the locker room, it's you. And I will go to Coach Roe about this. And I won't stop till your off the team. Because that's what we're supposed to be. A team. And you're not a part of that. Not now, not ever."

"Fuck you," Veronica spat, tears forming in her eyes. She grabbed her bag. "I don't need to put up with your shit." With that, she stormed off, Lisa trailing after her.

"Let her go," Miracle begged Lisa. Lisa paused as she looked back into the locker room.

"She's my friend, I'm sorry," Lisa said and ran after Veronica. I guess some people just didn't want help.

"Anyone else have a problem?" I asked the room. "Anyone want to say anything else? Please, go head before we have laps."

"That was cool, what you did. With how you reacted to the article," a pre-varsity cheerleader said.

"I hated that blog anyway," Del said with a shrug. "Ready to go?" I smiled and nodded as we all filed out. Maddie threw her arm around my shoulder. This was her first practice back since her injury.

"Ready? Three more practices left for field season," Maddie said. "Then we're done."

"I'm ready for homecoming," I said. "Can't believe you got cleared before the game."

"I know. Let's just make sure you're my spotter, okay?"

"Deal," I said, smiling. For the first time all season, I felt at home in cheer. They all knew who I was and that didn't change anything. I didn't realize how scared I was until the fear was proven to be false. I felt free.

ANDI

"Hey, Andi!" Maria called from the cash register. I was in the back going through the clearance books and making sure they all had the correct sticker. "Cat's here for you with dinner if you wanna take your break now."

"Oh, thanks!" I said and jumped up. Cat offered to bring me dinner and eat with me tonight because she didn't have practice on Wednesdays.

"Is she your friend?" Maria asked as she walked with me back to the front.

"Yes, but no, she's… She's my girlfriend," I said, looking away. Should I have said that?

"Oh, cool," she said. "She's here all the time. Let her know she can use your friends and family discount if you're dating."

"Yeah, she's a big reader, more than me, really," I said, smiling. "I'll let her know about the discount."

"Hey!" Cat said as I stepped out. She was holding a to-go bag.

"One sec, I gotta clock out," I said and went to the register.

"Be back in half an hour, okay?" Maria said. "I'm heading out so you gotta close with Josh."

"Got it," I said and gave her a thumbs up as I turned to Cat. "What'd you get us?"

"I got you a double bacon cheeseburger because you hate your heart," Cat teased. "And I got a veggie burger with bacon. Oh, and fries and I got you a Fanta in the car."

"A veggie burger with bacon?" I asked. Cat nodded.

"I didn't want the beef in the burger, it's too much meat," she explained. We got into her car and she turned it on and pushed her seat back so she could eat without her knees touching the wheel. "Oh, did you check Instagram?" Cat asked as she bit into her burger. I unwrapped mine, trying to be careful not to get any mayo on my uniform.

"No, what happened?" I asked. Cat smiled and handed me her phone. She's posted a photo of us from this morning. It was Barbie vs Ken Day. I just dressed in head-to-toe pink while she dressed up like a Barbie cheerleader. She'd put her hair in braids and was in a pink shirt that said BARBIE and a matching skirt. She also brought pink pom poms. Apparently, her cheer team had all agreed to wear the same outfit.

"Oh, also, Veronica is officially under investigation for cyber bullying," Cat said with a smile. "If she's found guilty, she'll have 5 days of OSS, and 5 days of ISS. And she'll be removed from the cheer team."

"Damn," I chuckled. "You really got her, babe."

"*We* really got her," Cat said. She looked out the window for a moment. "I do kinda feel bad—"

"Then don't. She made her own bed. Let her sleep in it."

"Yeah, but—"

"Nope." I said and threw a fry at Cat. She gasped and started laughing.

"If you get salt all over my car, I'm gonna be pissed," she said as she leaned over the cup holder to kiss me.

"Your hot when your pissed, that's not as big of a threat as you think it is," I said, making her laugh.

"Your terrible," Cat laughed.

"Yeah, but you love me so you put up with it," I said as she leaned over to kiss me.

CAT

Mickey met me outside of 5th period to walk me to lunch. "Hey, I wanna talk to you about something."

"What happened?" I asked. "Did someone say something to you? Is Andi—"

"I got asked out to homecoming," Mickey said. Oh. That wasn't what I was expecting.

"By a guy?"

"No, by a raccoon— Yes, by a guy," Mickey said sarcastically.

"Who?" I asked. "Oh my God, is it Aiden?"

"No," he said. "And your obsession with him and I is concerning. No, it's actually Ryan."

"Oh." I said. "Do you like him?" Ryan was totally his type, how did I not see this coming? And Ryan liked blondes. I knew they were friends; they'd known each other since middle school. But they mostly just played video games together at their own houses late at night after I'd logged off.

"Yeah," Mickey said. "Actually, him and I hooked up last Spring break."

"And you didn't tell me!"

"I thought you liked him! I didn't want you to know he and I hooked up!" Mickey said. "Plus, it was only, like, twice."

"I'll interrogate you about that later," I said. "But yeah, that's cool. He's a great guy. I'm happy for you, Mick."

"You sure it won't be uncomfortable?" He asked nervously.

"Dude, I'm with Andi. Ryan's not even an afterthought, he's not a thought. Do you need me to explain what being a lesbian means?" I asked sarcastically, making Mickey laugh.

"Okay, I didn't want it to be weird," Mickey said. "Yeah, I'm really excited. We started talking again after that beach party and we've been texting back and forth all the time."

"Hey, now I have someone I can go see your track meets with!" I said. I imagined Ryan and I getting up early to go see Mickeys 6 A. M. meets around Jacksonville.

"You could always take Andi," Mickey suggested.

"She is not a morning person," I said, smiling at the mental image of waking up with her in bed with me. "She'd hate getting up at 5."

"Everyone hates getting up at 5," Mickey said. "I don't know if Ryan will want to go."

"Oh, he'll go," I said. "I can't believe you two are gonna date—"

"We're just going to homecoming together, not getting married," Mickey sighed.

"Whatever, basically the same thing—"

"So totally not—"

"We should totally double date!" I said, holding onto Mickey's arm as we entered the cafeteria.

"I regret telling you already," Mickey said, laughing.

ANDI

"Why did we let them drive?" I said, shoving myself off of the car door after Rowan turned into the Goodwill.

"I legally got my license," Rowan said.

"And you're from Florida, it cancels out," Jordan said. "My dog could drive better then you, and he's missing an arm."

"We got here all in one piece."

"Barely!" Alex said, holding his head in his hand. Jordan turned around from the passenger seat.

"Are you okay?" They asked. "See, Rowan!"

"Nah, I'm fine," Alex said, rubbing his forehead. "Just hit my head against the window."

"I'm driving home," I said as we all got out of the truck. Rowan drove because Alex hates parking the truck. I think I'm just gonna help him practice parking it so he can drive us everywhere.

"Yes," Alex said, nodding. "Okay, I got 30 bucks for the outfit."

We were at Goodwill to get Alex a homecoming outfit. He wasn't sure if he wanted to go full suit or not. Jordan had gone out with their parents a few weeks ago and picked out a black dress. Rowan was going to wear dress pants and a shirt.

Rowan was the only one of us who'd ever gone suit shopping before. They led us to the men's isle and just started shoving clothes into Jordan's arm. Eight pairs of pants. Four shirts. Three vests.

"Wait, wait, this is so much," Alex said, trying to block Rowan from giving Jordan another pair of pants. "I did my measurements at home; we should use them."

"Then you're not accounting for the elastic ability of the fabric," Rowan stated matter-of-factly. "Trust me, I have a good eye with this shit."

"Okay," Alex said and walked over to me while Rowan went through any clothes that might fit him. "I can't wait for homecoming. Yours and Jordan's dresses look so nice."

"Thanks," I said. Rowan and Jordan were getting into an argument now over whether they should get a cart or not.

"I kinda wish I could get a dress," Alex said.

"Why?" I asked. Alex shrugged.

"I usually don't like dresses, but I like doing the cool hair and makeup. Can't do a lot with my hair, and I'd look out of place in a suit and eyeliner," Alex said.

"Rowan wears girls clothes and make up," I said.

"Yeah, but they're not trying not to be seen as a woman. I am," Alex said. "It's just with perception. The idea of a dress sounds cool because I think makeup is cool, but I'd never actually wear one."

"Do you wanna do my makeup? And hair?" Alex's face lit up.

"Really?" Alex asked excitedly. "I swear, I know what I'm doing."

"Yeah, I've seen you help Jordan out before competitions," I said. "I can come over a few hours before and you can do it and we can get ready together, deal?"

"Deal!" Alex said and hugged me. I hugged him back, smiling.

"Hey, Alex," Rowan said, coming over with a cart. "Go try this on and see what fits."

"Your such an ass, could you have worded that any ruder?" Jordan asked.

"Sorry," Rowan said, bowing and trying on a fake British accent. "Sir Alexander Wilson, would you do me the honor of downing on the garments Jordan and I have scavenged for you among the horrors of the Good Will?" They looked up, smirking. "That better, dearest?"

"Fuck off," Alex and Jordan said at the same time, causing all of us to laugh.

"I can go in with you and help," Jordan offered.

"No, you're not," Rowan said strictly. "He doesn't need you as a distraction."

"I'd help!" Jordan insisted, but Alex agreed with Rowan and instead let me into the changing room, along with the cart, to help him change in and out of the outfits. After what felt like hours of trying everything on, he found the perfect ensemble.

Alex stepped out in tan pants, a tan button up dress shirt, and a light pink floral blazer. "Holy shit, hon, you look amazing!" Jordan said and kissed him. Alex blushed and hid his face in Jordan's shoulder.

"See? You gotta try everything on," Rowan said, looking at the outfit proudly. "Okay, go change and we can check out."

Once Alex did, we paid and left. Rowan tried to make their way to the drivers' side, but I beat them to it. "Keys, Ricky Bobby," I said. Rowan rolled their eyes and handed me the keys.

CAT

"Go, Dolphins!" I yelled towards the bleachers. The sound of the crowd was deafening, but we were louder. Everyone cheered as Ryan ran the first touchdown of the night, making it 6:0.

We were up against some high school whose record was far worse than ours so it was a guaranteed win. Ryan did a victory bow and ran back to the benches to chug some Gatorade.

"Hey, Cat. Your girlfriend's waving at you," Miracle said, elbowing me. I beamed and turned around to see Andi leaning against the railing of the bleachers.

"Coach, can I—" I started to ask but she just smiled and nodded. I smiled back and dropped my pom-poms and ran up to the bleachers and stood on the benches against them so I was at eye level with Andi.

"Hey!' Andi said. Her breath came out like smoke because of how cold it was. We still had to be in our summer uniforms, so I was freezing. "I brought you some hot tea," she said, handing me a thermos.

"You're the best," I said, taking it from her. She was in her leather jacket, combat boots, blue jeans, and a green flannel. "It's only 60 degrees, why are you dressed like it's snowing?"

"I'm cold, fuck off," she laughed. "Your dressed like it's 90."

"Green!" Coach Roe called.

"Sorry, gotta go," I said. Before jumping off of the bench and running back, I leaned forward and pressed my lips to Andi's. They were cold and tasted like hot cocoa and peppermint.

There was no big cheer. Nobody was staring or watching us. I just got to kiss my girlfriend like it was a normal thing. It was perfect.

"Holy shit, we did it!" Ryan cheered as we drove to The Treehouse. They'd destroyed the other team, 27:6.

I was driving my group and Andi was driving hers. "I can't believe we're getting coffee instead of going to a real party," Maddie complained jokingly.

"Well, some of us don't wanna be hungover for homecoming," Mickey said from the passenger seat.

"Yeah, first school dance out," Maddie said. "Wait, is this all of our first school dance as being out?"

"I'm kinda out," Ryan said thoughtfully. "I mean, if anyone asked, I'd tell them I'm bi, but I don't really volunteer it."

"It's because he's embarrassed by me," Mickey said dramatically, leaning over the backseat to wink at Ryan.

"No, I'm not," Ryan said, taking Mickeys hand and kissing his knuckles. Mickey blushed and pulled his hand away, making Ryan laugh.

"Stop being so gay," Maddie complained sarcastically, making everyone laugh. "God, Ryan, I can't believe I thought you were straight."

"Thank you?" Ryan asked. I pulled into the parking spot and looked around the parking lot for Andi. I checked my phone and saw that Alex had texted that they'd be a little late because Jordan and Rowan left their wallets at Jordan's house 5 minutes away.

We all headed inside and got a table big enough for all of us and close to the karaoke machine. We all took turns getting drinks. I ordered mine and Andi's, and I noticed Ryan paid for Mickey's.

I watched a few karaoke performances while waiting on Andi. A couple did *Die With A Smile* together, but they sounded like they'd never heard the song before. It was pretty cute, though.

Some freshman did *You Belong with Me,* which got mixed reactions. I stood up and clapped for her. Fuck the people that hated Taylor Swift. Let people like what they like. Ryan clapped too, smiling at me from where he was sitting with Mickey.

"How are you an adult?" I heard someone complain and I turned to see Jordan, Rowan, Alex and Andi coming inside. Jordan and Rowan were bickering like always. Andi smiled and ran up to me and wrapped her arms around my neck.

"Are you cold?" She asked, pulling back. I shrugged. "Here, you can wear my jacket." I smiled as I slipped into her leather jacket. It smelt like her perfume.

"I got you a drink," I said and handed her a hot cocoa and matcha mix. She smiled and took it, taking a big sip.

"I really need the caffeine, thanks, babe," she said, standing on her toes to press a kiss to my cheek.

"Long day?" I asked. She nodded and sat on the sofa next to me and put her head on my shoulder. I wrapped my arm around her and drank my coffee.

Rowan did an excellent cover of *Taste* which made everyone laugh as they danced and sung to Alex. We spent the rest of the night drinking coffee and watching karaoke performances, curled up together in a booth.

It was normal. It was ordinary. It was perfect.

ANDI

Alex painstakingly curled my hair over the course of an hour. I'd cut my hair a few inches below my jaw a few days ago so it was harder to curl. I made a mental note to let it grow out for prom.

He was an artist with pins and hairspray. "This is bad for the environment," Rowan complained as they walked into the room as Alex was using hairspray.

"I will spray this in your eyes," Alex threatened. He had his own bedroom but Rowan usually hung out in his room, saying it was far cleaner than theirs.

"Want to order pizza?" Rowan asked as they laid down on Alex's bed.

"No," Alex said. "I still have leftovers from when we got Chinese that I need to eat before it goes bad."

"Andi?"

"No thanks," I said, trying not to move my head as Alex finished my hair. I was sitting in an office chair in a robe in front of his dresser mirror.

"Okay, now make up," Alex said.

"Wait, she should eat first. Andi, you need to eat something," Rowan said. "What about a PB&J?"

"That actually sounds really good," I said. Rowan got up. "I can make it."

"If you fuck up your hair, I'm pretty sure Alex will strangle me and not in a hot way," Rowan said and smiled at Alex. Alex scoffed and cross his hands over his chest making Rowan laugh. Rowan came back a minute later with two PB&Js for me and them and Alex's leftovers.

"Thanks." Alex said as they handed him the food. Rowan was sitting down on the floor to eat the PB&J. Alex had a stick no-food rule about his bed. Especially with Rowan. In fact, I was pretty sure the rule was made because of Rowan.

I finished the PB&J quickly and Alex did my makeup. I'd found some photos of smokey eyes off of Pinterest and Alex was trying his best to replicate them. After what felt like only ten minutes, Alex showed me my reflection.

"Damn, I look like I'm dating a rock star," I said. I looked amazing. My eyes were lined black and perfectly smudged with just the right amount of highlighter.

"Yeah, Alex, great fucking job, man," Rowan said, looking at my makeup as I pretended to pose.

"Thanks," Alex said. "I'm kicking you out so we can change." Rowan left to go change themselves as we got dressed. "Marcus and Jayma want to drive us to Cat's and then we'll take the Uber from there."

"Cool," I said as Alex helped me zip up the dress. I checked myself out in the mirror one more time. "Oh, can you hold my phone? I don't have pockets."

"Best thing about the suit," he said as he put my phone in his inside pocket. "Nine pockets, Andi. Nine."

Rowan meet us downstairs with Jordan. Jordan smiled and hugged Alex and kissed his cheek. "You look handsome," Jordan said, making Alex laugh and blush.

We spent half an hour just taking a bunch of photos. Jayma sent all of them to us before driving us to Cat's house. We were the last people there.

"Hey!" Cat yelled, running up to me as soon as I stepped out of the car. Her hair was ironed and her make up matched the light pink of her dress. She pulled me into a hug and kissed me quickly. "Wow," she said, looking me up and down. "You're gorgeous."

"You look stunning," I said reaching up to kiss her lips lightly. She still looked in shock to see me. "God, get your act together. We have photos, babe," I teased, taking her arm and walking with her to where our family was waiting for us.

Acknowledgements

I'd like to thank my amazing editor Caleb Diao who was the first person to ever read this book and gave me incredible advice on how to become a better author. This would not have been published without you.

I'd also like to thank my friends and family who put up with me talking about nothing but this book for the last 6 months before publishing. Specifically, my little sister, Bella, my mom, and my stepdad as well as my friends, Ruby, Rose, and Elliot. And of course, my brother, Zachary.

Thank you to all of the amazing teachers and librarians who always encouraged my love for books, reading, and storytelling.

Thank you to my grandparents who made sure I always had stories to read and tales to listen to. Thank you to my aunts for their support as well.

Finally, thank you to anyone who has read this book. This is truly a dream come true. If it's not obvious in the novel, I love books. I found who I was between the pages *of I'll Give You the Sun* and *When The Moon Was Ours*. I hope you, readers, found something that spoke to who you are as well.

I hope you love this novel as much as I do. Thank you for letting me live my dream.

ABOUT THE AUTHOR

Z.E. Lewis wrote this novel in 2024, the summer before their senior year of high school, and spent the year revising and editing it. It was published on their 18th birthday.

They were born in Charleston, South Carolina but grew up in Orange Park, Florida. They plan on attending UNF after high school graduation and majoring in Creative Writing.

As a queer teen growing up in Florida, they tried their best to write a honest story as well as a happy book for other queer teens that found who they were between the pages of a novel.

Made in the USA
Columbia, SC
19 February 2025

54107641R00164